UP IN FLAMES

No sooner had we pulled away than Latoya was laying into me.

"Jesus, not only do you attract the sheriff, you bring in the FBI!"

Benny pulled the car onto a dirt road, throwing me against the passenger door. Slamming the brakes, he came to a stop and I was pitched forward into the dash. Before I could move, he was on top of me, something cold and metallic jammed into my neck.

"Who are you?" I asked.

"Do what he says," Latoya said in a high, tight voice. "You don't want to know who he is."

I looked at the gun, then at Latoya. Her eyes were large and pleading.

"I told Edmonds about the money," I said. "About the money I took last year."

"Where is it?" Benny asked.

"It was in the cabin," I said. "The fire got it."

Berkley Prime Crime Books by Stephen J. Clark

SOUTHERN LATITUDES
DARK DELIVERY

DARK DELIVERY

STEPHEN J. CLARK

BERKLEY PRIME CRIME, NEW YORK

DARK DELIVERY

A Berkley Prime Crime Book / published by arrangement with the author

PRINTING HISTORY
Berkley Prime Crime mass-market edition / June 2003

For information address: The Berkley Publishing Group,
a division of Penguin Group (USA), Inc.,
375 Hudson Street, New York, New York 10014.

ISBN: 0-425-19110-9

Berkley Prime Crime Books are published by
The Berkley Publishing Group,
a division of Penguin Group (USA) Inc.,
375 Hudson Street, New York, New York 10014
The name BERKLEY PRIME CRIME and the
BERKLEY PRIME CRIME design
are trademarks belonging to Penguin Group (USA) Inc.

PRINTED IN THE UNITED STATES OF AMERICA

10 9 8 7 6 5 4 3 2 1

To my father, who gave me my first book,
Huck Finn

. . . what do you know of the dirt and the dark deliveries of the necessary? What do you know of dignity hard-achieved, and dignity lost through innocence, and dignity lost by sacrifice for a cause one cannot name. What do you know about getting fat against your will, and turning into a clown of an arriviste baron when you would rather be an eagle or a count or, rarest of all, some natural aristocrat from these damned democratic states. No, the only subject we share, you and I, is that species of perception which shows that if we are not loyal to our unendurable and most exigent inner light, then some day we may burn.

—Norman Mailer,
The Armies of the Night

BOOK 1

Evil draws men together.

—Aristotle,
Rhetoric

1

Ingram

THE night was all tumult, the trees blowing in the wind, lightning flashing in the distance as the first cold front of the season approached. I sat in the rocker on the screen porch, listening to the racket of the wind in the branches, peering into the dark and cradling my father's shotgun in my lap. It had been a long time since I had slept well, and rarely did I feel right without the gun within easy reach.

I had just come back from walking the perimeter of my property, stealing along the fence lines with the shotgun nestled in the crook of my arm. The woods around me had rustled and creaked as the wind whipped through the treetops. The air was still warm and full of the Gulf, but one could sense changes coming, the night electric, thunder rumbling in from points north.

As I had stood there along the fence, the droning of tires on pavement had come to my ears. I had crouched down beside the fence.

It was a throaty drone—truck tires. Out on the highway, I saw headlights telegraphing through the crisscross of trees.

I pulled myself into the shadow of a scrub oak, although I must have been thirty yards deep in the woods. The lights grew larger, the tires droning louder. For a moment the headlights caught me clean in the face, then the truck ripped past, pinpoints of red now receding through the trees.

Just another good-ol'-boy rolling home.

I stood and breathed again. It's on a night like this that I imagine them coming back—pulling up along the shoulder of the road and creeping through the woods. After a minute, I moved along, two drinks past drunk, just another good-ol'-boy myself limping on home.

IT had been more than a year since I had stumbled into the biggest mess of my life as a down-on-my-luck newspaper reporter working for the little daily paper in my backwater of a hometown. Having blundered into a money-laundering pipeline funneling mob drug dollars out of the country, I had nearly gotten myself and several others killed, and had ended up with a pilfered box of their money, and the hope that my name would not find its way back to the criminal Powers-That-Be. Although the sum of my knowledge of organized crime stemmed from an appreciation of the films of Coppola, Scorcese, and De-Palma, I was relatively certain that this was a faint hope. Any man with an instinct for self-preservation would have long since departed for points far afield—preferably some lost patch of Alaskan tundra—but instead, I had remained here in my own Potter County, stranded by trepidation and inertia.

The silhouette of my father's river cabin loomed over

me as I approached, perched twenty feet in the air on poles as protection against the spring floods. I walked up the creaky steps and inside.

This had been my home for more than a year now—the mildewed, dusty shack that my father had built twenty-five years ago. I closed and locked the door and went to the fridge for more ice to float in my next double of George Dickel.

Turning off all the lights, I sat in one of the porch rockers, listening to the storm descend upon me, the shotgun in my lap, reflecting on the fact that the older we get, the more like ourselves we become. A year ago, I had come back home after twenty years away and had felt that at the end of it all I had found myself and buried not a few ghosts. But despite hard-won insights, bitter resolutions, and a dedication to change oneself for the better, character and old habits have a way of reasserting themselves. You intend to improve your lot, eat better, start jogging, and volunteer to help the poor, but somehow events distract you, time cannot be found, and the television always beckons with another episode of *Fantasy Island*. You may instead leave behind all that you owned, travel halfway across the world, take up residence among an alien people intending to begin again, but you awaken in the morning to find that you are still your same cursed self. So, after the bloody ordeal of last year, after a naked reappraisal of the wreckage that was my life and career, after the most profound resolution to change and grow, I found myself deadended again, stuck on the screen porch of this dilapidated river house, doling out cash from my box of stolen money, marking time only by my weekly runs into town to stock up on frozen dinners and whiskey, and by the sluggish change of the seasons here in Alabama's backwoods, all the while looking over my shoulder for the inevitable dropping of the second shoe.

I rocked and stared out into the night. Soon the thunderstorms would blow in, and the wind would shift around from the north and the temperature drop twenty degrees in an hour. Although this would be a break from the summer's heat, I did not greet it with any joy, for it served as the first warning of the winter to come. Last year I had spent too many nights freezing in this leaky cabin as the cold swept in between the loose lath.

It was somewhere past two in the morning when I went to bed. Lying on the moldy mattress, wrapped in old blankets, I tried to find sleep, surrounded as always by memories of my father. This has been his beloved fishing camp, where he'd escaped the stresses and conundrums of his life, and where he'd died his ignominious and drunken death. Upon my return here, I'd settled in amid the dreadful reminders of him. My whole life seemed as if it had occurred in the shadow of his conflicted life and passing.

I heard a rattling. It was only the slightest of noises, but it came to my ears through the storm's backdrop as piercing and known as the cry of one's own child.

In an instant, I rolled back out of the bed and knelt on the floor, holding the shotgun aimed at the open doorway. I thumbed the safety off and hunkered down behind the bed, alert in an instant, peering through the dark, listening and scared shitless.

Just a raccoon, I told myself, or maybe a rat.

I stood and moved quickly from the bedroom to the kitchen, grabbing my Mag-Lite off the counter. Using the kitchen counter as cover, I peered around the front room. I could hear the wind tearing through the trees and shaking the tin roof. Then it came again—a rattling.

The knob of the front door jiggled back and forth. I brought the shotgun up and trained it on the door. The knob jiggled again.

My heart fluttered in my chest. Creeping around the

counter, I made my way to the wall beside the door. My shoulder to the wall, I kept the gun trained on the door, crouching low.

What was I going to do? Fling open the door and let fly? Cower here against the wall and pray?

I slid backward along the wall and lay along the floor, the shotgun trained on the door. Anyone who came in would have to answer to the Mossberg.

The phone rang. My heart came all the way up in my chest and threatened to burst free.

It rang again, the sound almost as jolting as the first ring. The creak of footfalls descending the front steps followed. The phone rang again. I stood and pulled back the blinds on the window beside the door. A silhouette stole away from the house and into the woods.

The phone rang for the fourth time. I moved into the bedroom and picked it up off the bedside table.

"Ingram," I said. "This better be good."

"Nelson?" the voice on the other end said. "It's Jack—Jack Edmonds."

"Jack? Do you have any idea what time it is?" Jack Edmonds was a friend from my days as a reporter in Richmond. He was a special agent with the FBI who had been involved in cleaning up the mess I made here last year.

"Yeah," he said, "It's almost three A.M. I just got the call myself. That crooked sheriff who got you in trouble down there last year—that Stanton fellow—has just turned up dead down in the bayou country south of New Orleans."

I hunkered lower beside the bed, eyeing the doors and windows. "No shit?"

"We've been looking for him ever since he lit out from your environs. Unfortunately, somebody else got to him first."

"Somebody just tried to break in here," I said. "Just a

minute ago. When the phone rang, they got spooked and ran off."

"I don't think it was the neighbors coming with coffee cake," Jack said. "You still out at that damn river cabin?"

"Yeah."

"Listen," he went on, "I don't know what's going on there, but the people you messed with last year had friends and families, and those guys have a history of carrying big grudges."

"What do I do?" I asked.

"Sit tight. I'll be in touch later today. If anyone comes back tonight, call 911."

"Yeah. Like the sheriffs are going to rush right out here after what I put them through last year."

"They'll come. They know we're still watching."

"Why are you still involved in this, Jack?" I asked.

"I got you to thank for that," he said. "After you dumped this case in my lap, the Bureau made me Special Agent In-Charge. Why do you think they're calling me at this hour?"

"Congratulations," I said.

"Yeah. Got me transferred from D.C. to goddamn Birmingham. Congratu-fucking-lations. I'll talk to you later," he said and hung up the phone.

The line went dead and the dial tone came up. Wrapped in a blanket, I sat on the floor beside the bed, trying to wish away this nightmare. I climbed back into bed and lay the shotgun on the floor along the wall. I slept fitfully and uneasily with torpid dreams, waking with every creak or tick of the cabin. It seemed like dawn would never come.

2

L̲ATE summer stumbled its way toward autumn. An old man of seventy-five, bones riddled with cancer, I did not welcome the coming of colder weather. Toward the end of September, the first Canadian front finally conquered the warmer air from the Gulf and pushed on through the state. It had rained sometime past midnight and in the morning the gray-white skies of summer had given way to a deep blue, the humidity in the air replaced by a gracious dryness. A cool breeze flowed in from the north.

I awoke on these cool mornings with aged joints as rigid as rigor mortis, a gnawing pain deep in the bones of my back. The sun had yet to clear the horizon. The Canadian breeze riffled through the leaves and Lacy's wind chimes. A blue jay cackled. I lay in bed, taking account of myself. Lungs working well despite more than a half-century of smoking. It seemed that I was still in my right mind. Everything moved, albeit painfully. I held out my hand, staring at the thin skin showing the web of veins and the tented runs of tendon from forearm to hand, the swollen joints creaking and popping as I flexed and opened the hand.

What a piece of work—the hand!

What a bitch it was being old.

Thirty minutes earlier I had taken 10 milligrams of morphine, and now I felt its warm glow, the gnawing pain in my back fading to a distant ache. I pitched back the covers and rolled to the floor, falling to my knees beside the bed. From here, I could push up with my hands and stand. The pain was electric but fleeting as I stood and squared my hips under me.

I walked to the door and opened it. A cool breeze wafted in, riffling my hair. The sky was a deep rinsed cobalt blue, a high fringe of frozen cirrus pushing in from the north on the winds. The meadow was damp with the night's rain. A covey of quail fed at its far end.

I laughed aloud. Prostate cancer, gnawing pain, wasted body, and morphine aside, it was good to be here on this autumn morning. I laughed and shook my head in bewilderment. Damn you, Lord, but I've made it to see another day in your beautiful, goddamned, godforsaken world.

I went to the bathroom sink and took 60 milligrams of the MS Contin—a time-release morphine that would hopefully keep the pain dialed down to a dull roar all day long. It lacked the pleasing rush of the short-acting stuff. One barely noticed it after a few doses, but it did the job and allowed me to pass as a shambling corpse-to-be among the living. If it weren't for the damned constipation, I could almost believe that the drugs made such a life bearable.

From the kitchen I smelled the coffee brewing. It was still a good smell. I inhaled it greedily. Drinking it was another matter. Most mornings this, too, was a small pleasure, but sometimes it would bring on waves of nausea that had me kneeling before the toilet bowl savoring instead stomach acid and bile as it all came back up. Such mornings were enough to abort the whole day. I would take to my bed with a Compazine suppository and nod away into afternoon in a drugged sleep. Coffee was a gamble, but one that I still undertook. I pulled on my old gray sweats, yanked the drawstring tight around my shrinking waist, and made my way to the kitchen.

William waited in the kitchen, sitting at the breakfast table with the newspaper. He looked up as I entered, regarding me over his reading glasses.

"Mornin', Dr. Hartley."

"Morning, William."

William was the husband of my wife's housekeeper, Ella Mae. Over the years he had evolved into an appendage of Ella Mae around the house. When Lacy became ill with her breast cancer, they both moved into the house to help with her care. Lacy died within a year and Ella Mae went soon after—a pulmonary embolus followed by a heart attack. That left William and me staring at each other in this big empty house, two dazed widowers. William had nowhere to go and I had no one else left in the world. He made an effort to fill Ella Mae's role, but he was as beside himself as me. I went back to work after a couple of weeks. William settled in, becoming a sort of Man Friday. He kept the place clean, became a creditable Southern cook, and began clothing himself out of the *L.L. Bean* and *Lands' End* catalogs.

Sitting now at the breakfast table in khaki slacks, a plaid shirt, and Bean topsiders, he looked like a retired professor from Alabama A & M. He had only a high school education, but since moving in, he had begun working his way through my library. He had even begun, self-consciously, to try to lose his Alabama accent, deliberately overpronouncing words, making an obvious effort to say "ask" instead of "aks," "library" instead of "libree," "can't" instead of "caint," and so on.

I don't know what I would have done without him over these past few years, especially since the cancer had begun to hit me hard. But I'm afraid that years of living with an overeducated, disaffected white man had changed him in ways that were not to his benefit. Among whites he would always be a poor black handyman, no matter how well he dressed or spoke. Out in society, he must mind his place and position, avert his eyes when talking to society women of a certain sort, laugh excessively at the jokes of white folk, smile and play the fool when necessary. Among his fellow blacks, he was doubtlessly seen as uppity, odd, and distant. He was a good and honest man and I owed him much.

He watched me move gingerly into the kitchen. "How're you doing this morning?" he asked, assaying me like a piece of bad meat.

"Tolerable, William," I said, pouring myself some coffee. It tasted preternaturally good this morning.

"What you think about this weather?" he asked.

"Always loved fall, but the cold really gets to me these days."

" 'Spect so. Can I get you some breakfast? A poached egg and some grits?"

"Thanks, but no. Stomach still feels a bit rocky."

William stared at me, then shook his head. "Practically skin and bones as it is. I don't know how I'm gonna get any meat back on you."

"Sorry, William. I'll try some of that loco weed of yours this afternoon and we'll see how I can do with dinner."

William grunted skeptically. About six months ago he had brought me some marijuana. Despite my prejudices, I had to admit that it took the edge off my nausea and helped me keep food down.

A cardinal, a bright red male, perched at the bird feeder outside the kitchen window. In the slanting morning light amid the dark green leaves of early autumn, he seemed too vivid, too colorful to exist—like a visiting spirit. William and I watched him perch there. Then, on a tree past the feeder, a large pileated woodpecker flapped into view and lighted on the trunk. His red crest flared brighter than the cardinal, he swiveled his head back and forth, seeming to cast his gaze upon us.

"Look at that big son of a gun," William said, "My momma used to call them 'Lord Gods' cause of the way their call sounds coming to you way far off through the woods."

He was a lordly son of a bitch. He clung there to one of my scrub pines, pecking at the tree, his blank reptilian ball-bearing eyes goggling to and fro. Like so much of creation, he was majestic and indifferent. Nature's beauty was a tease, a cheat, just window-dressing cheering up an otherwise bleak view.

"William, get me my gun so I can shoot that son of a bitch."

"What kinda talk is that? You want to shoot that beautiful bird? Think that bird got so big and beautiful by letting old farts like you take shots at it?"

A splash of bile visited the back of my throat. I harrumphed and reached for some of the newspaper.

"You just in a bad mood 'cause your back's hurting you," he said.

I disdained to answer, opening the newspaper. That privileged peckerwood Bush looked like he was going to whip that Greek peckerwood Dukakis.

"Got therapy today?" William asked.

God, but William could be a pest sometimes. "Same time as every day for the last two weeks," I said.

William grunted in affirmation, ignoring the rebuke in my voice, studying the newspaper through his reading glasses.

"You want me to drive you?" he asked at last, not looking up.

"I think I'll be okay."

AT ten-thirty I drove myself over to the Cancer Center in Tuscaloosa. A few weeks ago I had finally broken down and told Pavel, my urologist, about the gnawing pains at the base of my spine. He was a burly Polish Catholic from Long Island who had moved down here to escape the wretched Northeast and to carpet-bag off us poor, dumb Southerners. He exploded into the examination room smiling, glad-handing, one fleshy hand massaging my shoulder, appraising it unconsciously for the meat on my bones and tone of my muscles, full of the joy of ministering to the kidney and prostate and urinary troubles of old and young. In three minutes he had rapped up and down my back, put his finger on my stony hard prostate, told me what I already knew — that he thought the cancer had spread to my spine — ordered a bone scan, commiserated at what a bitch life could be, gave me a follow-up appointment, and sent me on my way.

The bone scan showed the black blotches of tumor spread up and down my spine. Another three-minute visit with Dr. P. gave me one more drink from the milk of human kindness, a prescription for the morphine, a Lupron shot, and a referral to a radiation oncologist.

"Jeez, this is a bitch, Seymour," Pavel said, writing out the prescription. "You know you shoulda let me take that prostate out five years ago when we first found that lump."

"So I could have spent the last five years impotent and dribbling into my Depends?"

Pavel shrugged. "Yeah, well, that happens sometimes."

"No regrets," I said. "I'm seventy-five and I'm getting tired."

Where Pavel was a rotund, sweaty, bustling whirlwind, Dominguez, the radiation oncologist, was a slender, precise second-generation Miami Cuban who sat behind his oak desk in a starched white lab coat, holding a Mont Blanc fountain pen while he spoke of radiation ports and centigray and partial remission rates. It seemed as far removed from my own health as if we had been discussing orbital trajectories for the space shuttle. They had me climb into a hospital gown, painted my body to label the radiation ports, strapped me to a gurney, and then tracked me underneath their great humming machines. The only outward stigmata I bore were the port markers and a modest sunburn where the beam passed through the skin.

The real price was higher. There is a subtle adjustment of the psyche that occurs when one becomes a *patient*, an insidious stripping of dignity through minutes dribbled away sitting in holding rooms naked except for the gown that leaves your ass flapping, lying passively while strong hands move you, while an electric gantry trundles you about, while disembodied voices tell you when to breathe and not to breathe, when you may come and when you have leave to go. By degrees you sink into a demoralized state that threatens to invade the rest of your life. Even after you've dressed again in your street clothes and left the hospital, you walk with a mincing, short-strided gait. You scan the streets, searching for dangers that are not there, second-guess yourself, avoid decisions, and look forward to the afternoon naps you've started taking. In short, you become the dithering old fart you've spent years fighting off.

As a result, after each radiation session, I felt obliged to commit some minor act of rebellion. Usually this meant driving down to The Men's Club out past the county line down along the Interstate on the way back from Tuscaloosa, and having a shot and a beer while smoking several cigarettes and watching naked girls writhe around on a brass pole. Lacy had made me promise never to drink until after 5 P.M., my internist had made me quit smoking, and no one in the Hartley clan had ever been in a strip joint outside of New Orleans or Havana; but there I was, tossing back Jack Daniels and Budweiser, smoking Pall Malls, watching tits and ass, and feeling low and ornery. Each day, it seemed to take a little longer to recover myself from the experience in the hospital. That day it was two rounds, six cigarettes, and two strippers to do the requisite work.

The bartender was an anonymous fellow who wore Sansabelt polyesters and bowling shirts. He didn't know quite what to make of an old geezer at his bar drinking heavily just past noon, but had the wisdom to let me alone. The girls on the stage were testament to the quality and profligacy of God's handiwork, and the unworthiness of man—beautiful bodies full in the breast, ample in the bottom, and long in the thigh, yet thrown into this dim cesspool like so many empty beer cans. What was the Lord thinking when he made so many of these lovely girls that to us they became as discounted and hard worn as an old dollar? What were we thinking when we allowed these divine confluences of muscle and tendon and flesh to be so badly used?

An hour was enough to stoke my ire and spite back to normal levels. I went back out into the day. It had turned into a beautiful fall afternoon. As I drove the Suburban toward home, the first leaves beginning to turn, the air possessed of a clarity that sharpened colors and made each object seem distinct and vivid, the light with that long, slanting quality that you see between the equinox and the solstice, I felt young again, reminded of autumns from fifty and sixty years ago—football weekends with my father, listening to the Crimson Tide on the radio or making the trip into Tuscaloosa for the game, hunting weekends walking through autumnal fields or hunkering in a duck blind at dawn relishing the cold that seemed to seep up out of the marshy ground like a memory of the last winter. For the first time in days I felt whole and all of a piece. Air flowed full into my lungs, and I could feel my diaphragm working easily. I leaned my head out the open window of the truck and let the wind hit me square in the face, feeling the sun warm like an old hound dog leaning out from the back of a pickup.

I pulled into the driveway and drove up to the garage. I climbed out. There was no pain in my back. My shoulders felt loose. I walked with a spring in my step. Perhaps that radiation was helping after all.

Opening the front door, I stood in the entry hall. The house was unnaturally quiet. I looked into the living room. The coffee table was overturned. The drawers of the hutch were all pulled out, their contents strewn about. A lamp lay on the floor.

"William?" I called aloud.

The compressor on the refrigerator came on.

"William?" I walked carefully through the living room and into the kitchen.

In the kitchen, cabinets had been opened, drawers pulled out and scattered. The place had been ransacked.

I went to my bedroom and pulled the 9mm Glock from beneath the mattress. The magazine was in. I jacked a round into the chamber and clicked the safety off.

Kneeling by the bedside table, I held myself still and listened. I could hear the faint rumble of the refrigerator in the kitchen, the wind in the trees outside. I heard something drip in the bathroom. I stood and moved slowly toward the open bathroom door.

I saw the feet and legs in the doorway. The body lay prone alongside the tub, a pool of blood drying on the white tile floor. I knelt over it, lay down the gun, and rolled the body over.

It was William.

I checked the carotid.

Nothing.

I pulled him onto his back and tore open his shirt. An entry wound lay just to the left of his sternum. I let out a cry, visceral pain, as if I felt the wound myself. I lay my ear on his bloodied chest and listened.

Nothing.

I grabbed his shirt and shook him, as if this would rouse him.

"Goddamnit! William, you can't do this."

I rolled off the body and slumped against the doorjamb. All the oxygen had left the room. I gasped for air. The bathroom stank of the sweet ferric smell of blood. William lay twisted on the floor. From the look of his face, he had been beaten before they killed him.

Who could have done this?

Then it came to me. This had to do with Ingram and all the murderous shit he had gotten me involved in last year.

3

I SLEPT badly, thrashing in the damp sheets, waking
every few minutes to peer at the clock and the door and
nothing at all. Finally, as dawn begin to creep up the sky, I
was able to sleep soundly.

This was my habit. In the night I had dreams of falling
and nightmares about dread and the keening of imminent
disaster and did not know which I feared more—the stuff
of my dreams or the threat of what lurked outside my door.
Daylight brought an illusory security to things, though,
and I found that with it I could usually get a few hours of
sleep in those quiet early morning hours.

I had dreamt of my father. We were on a trip to Washington, D.C., standing in the Smithsonian looking up at the
Spirit of St. Louis. He stood towering over me there, contemplating the airplane, his face grim. Finally he spoke as
if from deep within a well. "Lindbergh was a blessed fool.
He had no idea of the risks he was taking. It was better that

way. If he had known half of what could have gone wrong, he'd have never even taken the plane out of the hangar." He stalked my nights as he had my days. My selfish, vagrant, and indifferent life had been a reaction to his consuming, self-destructive righteousness. My mostly vain attempt to mimic his bravery since my return had only left me marooned, still under his spell, but high and dry and uncertain as to how to proceed, haunted by *déjà vus* and genuine dread.

It was the phone that tore me from sleep. I started awake with its ring, reaching down for the shotgun in the instant I opened my eyes, my heart pounding, eyes gritty, my head aching from the usual hangover. I was twisted up in the sweaty sheets.

I blinked as I pulled the shotgun to me. The room was empty. For a moment I couldn't remember what had awakened me. The image and sound of my father lingered in my mind like a bitter aftertaste. The phone rang a second time, the sound piercing and painful.

I put the gun back on the floor and reached for the phone. It rang again before I could get to it. The sound was so jarring that I batted the receiver off just to stop it. It clattered to the floor, making a noise that was only a little easier to bear.

Bleary-eyed, I hunted for the receiver. Finally I found the phone cord and followed it as it ran under the bed, pulling the receiver out with it. At last I brought it to my ear.

"Hello?" I said, my voice still thick with sleep.

"Gawd-damn, what're you doing out there?" It was Sonny Trottman, former high school classmate and sergeant for the Litchfield Police Department.

"Hey, Sonny," I said.

"You still asleep, Nelson?" he asked. "Hell's Bells! It's almost three o'clock."

"Kinda had a late night," I said feebly.

"Jesus," he said. "Ever since you retired out to that damn shack out at the river, you haven't been worth two goddamns."

Somehow, in the wake of last year, Sonny had been misconstrued as having played some role in actually "cracking the case." As a result, he had been rescued from his exile on the night shift and now had the job of dayshift watch commander. Besides allowing him to now sleep at night, this august title also apparently gave him the right to preach to me, as his station in life had now eclipsed my own.

"Someone tried to break into my place last night," I said. "It was hard to get to sleep after that."

"Well, forget about that," Sonny said. "You need to get your ass out of bed and get dressed. Seymour Hartley's housekeeper was murdered this morning."

"William?" I asked.

"Hartley's still out at the house. All he can say is, 'Fucking Ingram, goddamn fucking Ingram!' You need to get out there, Nelson. With William Charles gone, he don't have nobody left in the whole damn world."

"Okay," I said, grappling with the news. "I'm on my way."

"The place is covered up with cops," Sonny said. "Just tell 'em I sent you."

"Okay," I said and hung up.

I dressed hurriedly, pulling on yesterday's clothes and splashing my face with water. I carried the Mossberg with me as I left the house. On the front landing I looked at the doorjamb and knob but couldn't see any signs of the prowler from last night. I turned and scanned the lot. Nothing unusual.

The rain had passed through in the night and now the air had a washed, northern crispness, the light clear and

golden. Autumn had rolled into Potter County. But the bad
night, the dreadful news, and the remnants of the dreams
of my father persisted, coloring things with presentiments
of doom.

My father had died drunk in a hunting accident when I
was twelve years old, leaving me in the hands of my
drunken mother. That trip to Washington with my father
had occurred a month before he died. On a half-day's notice, he'd decided I needed to see our nation's capital. My
mother was glad to be rid of us. He'd been deep into himself for months, withdrawn and drinking hard. Things had
been going badly for him with his law practice. My mother
and he barely spoke anymore. The trip had seemed like an
impulsive, out-of-character notion. After a fit of manic
packing, we set off on the road in the morning. My father's
good spirits lasted about a hundred miles. Then the grim-
ness settled back upon him like a fog, the miles of blank
road seeming to drain him until he seemed as lifeless as a
week-old party balloon. With the radio off, the only sound
had been the droning of the tires on the road. Looking up
at him, I felt only confusion and a terrible sinking in my
gut, not sure what was going to become of him or me.

Perhaps my memory had been colored by subsequent
events, but the sense of foreboding and loss seemed to per-
meate that journey, and its recollection through dream now
hung over this day. To start the day with news of murder,
then, seemed perfectly in keeping.

I had taken to parking my car on the neighboring lot
hidden in some bushes so that the cabin would look unin-
habited to passers-by. To get to the car now I had to hike
all the way across my lot, hop a wire fence, and then hike
again to the center of the next lot. This tract belonged to
Georgia-Pacific and was populated only with a run of
evenly spaced pines all about ten years old.

Hubert, the doughty LTD that Uncle Rayburn had given

me when I first came to Litchfield, waited among the brambles at the end of the dirt road that ran across the lot. Some branches had fallen across its hood during the storm last night. I cleared them off and stood for a moment beside the car, the shotgun riding in the crook of my arm, surveying the ground around me.

A breeze rustled the leaves in the treetops. Nothing stirred save the blue jays that crashed around in the branches. Beyond the far property line, about a hundred yards away I could make out the cabin of my nearest neighbor—a rudimentary shack on a low foundation. A tall, dark-complexioned fellow had lived there for almost a year now. I had seen him from a distance through the trees now and then.

I climbed in Hubert and cranked the engine over. Reluctantly, it started and I backed out to the main highway and headed toward Hartley's house.

Our two houses could not have been farther apart and still have remained in the same county. My little cabin lay at the northeast end of the county, high up on the Sour Mash River above Lake Litchfield. His home was at the southern terminus of the county, just above where the Sour Mash flowed into the Tennessee-Tombigbee Waterway.

Traveling the forty miles on the winding, two-lane county roads took almost an hour. When I pulled down the gravel drive that led to his house, I found it clogged with police cars.

A couple of officers stood on the front steps of the house, surveying the front yard with a professional detachment. They eyed me suspiciously as I parked my battered LTD on the far side of the knot of cars and climbed out. I waved and smiled, trying my best to appear unthreatening, but they would have none of it.

"This here's a crime scene, mister," one of them said in

a thick Alabama drawl. "Afraid you're gonna have to move along."

"I'm a friend of Dr. Hartley's," I said. "Sonny Trottman asked me to come down here."

The other officer looked me up and down.

"Hey, Nelson," he said in an even thicker drawl. It was Bobbie Majors, Sonny's old partner, still a beanpole in an oversized uniform. If Sonny's unearned fame from last year's exploits had catapulted him into a heady leadership role, then Bobbie had at least parlayed his association with Sonny into a day-shift job.

"Hey, Bobbie," I said, trying to stretch my atrophic drawl to match his. "What's going on here?"

Bobby rolled his eyes. "Gawd," he said, "It's a terrible mess in there. Poor William Charles is all over the master bathroom."

"What happened?" Old reporter's habits died hard as I pumped him for information.

"Shot dead through the chest," Bobby said.

I nodded and moved past them and into the house. Things were in a tumult, overturned chairs in the living room, drawers pulled out and their contents spilled across the floor. I followed the murmur of voices into the master bedroom. Chief of Police Bailey sat on the bed beside an old man who hunched forward staring at the floor.

"Fucking Ingram," the old man said. When he spoke, I recognized him as Dr. Hartley. He had aged tremendously since I had last seen him, a frail stick of a man now.

They looked up at me as if I had been conjured by the invocation of my name. Hartley didn't seem to recognize me at first, his tired, red eyes regarding me quizzically. Then his gaze narrowed.

"Goddamn Nelson Ingram," he said. "This is all your doing." He rose and advanced on me, a bony fist balled up and held ready at his side.

Chief Bailey reached out to restrain him, saying, "Simmer down, Seymour."

But Hartley pulled away from him and closed the space between us. "This is all on your head," he said, his face close up to mine.

"I know," I said. "I'm sorry." He held my gaze and I didn't look away. "I'm sorry," I said again.

He held my gaze another beat. "Damn right you should be sorry," he said at last and lowered his fist.

He turned and sat down in the chair across from the bed. "My own damn fault for ever listening to you. Your last name was Ingram, I should've known better. Suicidal crusades are an Ingram tradition. Your father about destroyed this whole damn town with his."

I sat on the bed opposite him. "What happened?" I asked.

"What happened?!" he asked, growing heated again. "What the hell do you think happened?"

Chief Bailey was at my side. "He found William Charles on the bathroom floor. The house had been ransacked."

"Shot through the goddamn chest," Hartley said.

"And who would *they* be?" I asked.

"That's what we'd like to know," Bailey said.

Bailey and Hartley were staring at me. "What?" I asked.

Bailey cleared his throat. "Well, in the light of some of your past . . . dealings, we thought you might know who could be behind this."

I looked around the room, feeling suddenly embarrassed.

"Well," I said, playing for time, "I did hear from one of my friends at the FBI last night . . ."

Everyone continued to stare.

"And he told me that they found Harold Stanton murdered down in Louisiana."

"Stanton?" Hartley asked. "That sheriff we ran off last year?"

"His place was ransacked pretty much like this, too," a deep voice came from the open door to the room.

In walked Jack Edmonds—a tall, reserved black man in a well-cut dark suit. He scanned the room then nodded in the direction of Chief Bailey, reaching out to shake his hand.

"Jack Edmonds," he said. "FBI."

Bailey knew him from last year. "Sure," he said, smiling uneasily. "Special Agent Edmonds. What brings you down this way?"

"This," he said, gesturing around the room.

"Homicide?" Bailey said. "It's a local matter."

Jack smiled painfully. "Since my friend Nelson here got me involved in this last year, as you recall, I've been appointed Special Agent In-Charge of the follow-up investigation. I'm afraid this falls under follow-up."

"Guess we all got something to thank Ingram for," Hartley said ironically.

"I drove in from Birmingham this morning," Jack said. He walked professionally around the bedroom then peered into the bathroom, where a couple of officers were still photographing and dusting the scene.

"Where's the body?" he asked.

"They took it about a half hour ago," Bailey said quietly.

Hartley looked up at Edmonds, steely-eyed. "Entry wound anterior chest, midclavicular line at about T-5 consistent with a large-caliber handgun," he said. "Powder burns on the clothing. No exit wound. By the amount of bleeding I'd say the round missed the heart but disrupted the great vessels. Death by exsanguination."

Edmonds raised an eyebrow. "Dr. Hartley, as I recall?"

Hartley nodded.

"The pathologist?"

"Retired."

"This is your house?"

"And he was my friend. Now are you going to tell me who killed him?"

Jack circled back to the middle of the bedroom to stand opposite Hartley, who still sat in the overstuffed chair in the corner. "It would just be conjecture at this point," he said.

"Conjecture away," Hartley said, "Because if you don't tell me something that sounds pretty damn good, I'm going looking for those bastards myself."

Jack shot a sleeve out and fiddled with his tie. He wasn't used to working such a hostile room.

"Well, what with Stanton showing up dead, you've got to suspect that our friends in organized crime are looking for payback. They may have finally figured out who queered their operation down here."

"Someone tried to break into my place last night," I said.

"They worked on Stanton for quite a while before they killed him," Jack went on. "Ransacked his place even worse than here and probably tortured him for a good while to boot. They may have gotten your names out of him."

"Why didn't you warn us?" Hartley asked.

"I called Nelson as soon as I got word of it," Jack said.

"I was going to call you today," I said to Hartley, "but—"

"But you slept past goddamn noon again," Hartley said disgustedly.

"I don't think it's safe for you two to stay around here," Jack said. "Whoever killed Mr. Charles will likely be back looking for the one or the both of you."

"I'm not leaving my house," Hartley said.

"Seymour," Bailey said, "We can provide protection for a day or two, but we can't do it indefinitely."

Edmonds had circled back to the doorway of the bathroom and studied the officers gathering evidence. He turned to Chief Bailey. "Listen, Chief," he said, searching for tact, "I can have an evidence team here in a couple of hours. What do you say we leave the scene to them?"

Bailey looked him in the eyes, saying nothing.

"This crime relates to an ongoing federal investigation," Edmonds said. "Not that your boys don't know their jobs, but I'm sure we can bring more resources to bear here and we'll share all information fully."

Bailey held his gaze then sighed and nodded. "Boys," he called into the bathroom, "let's leave the scene as it is for now. FBI's on the way."

One of the officers stuck his head out of the bathroom, looking from the Chief to Edmonds and back.

"Just do it," Bailey said.

"Okay, Chief," the officer said.

"I'm not moving," Hartley said again.

Bailey turned to Hartley. "Seymour—" he began.

"Dr. Hartley," Edmonds interrupted, coming in between the two, "Your house is going to be covered up all day with FBI and police. It's not practical for you to stay here. We can put you up somewhere you'll be safe."

"He can stay with me," I said.

They all turned to look at me.

"You just got done saying that someone tried to break into your place last night," Edmonds said. "Do you realize it could be the same people?"

"No, that'll be fine," Hartley said. He stood. "C'mon, Nelson, let's go."

"I don't think that would be wise," Edmonds said.

"Nonsense," Hartley said, "We'll be fine." He pulled a

canvas duffel from his closet, tossed it onto his bed, and began throwing some clothes into it.

Edmonds turned to Bailey, his look asking if everyone down here was crazy. Bailey pulled his mouth to one side in a smile and shook his head. "Now, look, Seymour," he said.

"Don't 'Look, Seymour' me!" Hartley said. "If you people had been doing your job, those mafia bastards would have never set up shop here, then Nelson would have never gotten involved with them and I'd have just minded my own business and William'd be alive right now."

He zipped up his duffel and walked past both of them. "Now get your ass moving and let's get going," he said to me.

I stood and looked at Edmonds and Bailey.

Hartley was halfway out the door, his duffel over his shoulder. "Goddamnit, Ingram," he said, "I'm not getting any younger."

I shook my head at Edmonds and followed him out.

Hartley was already headed into the kitchen when I caught up with him.

"Are you sure this is a good idea?" I asked, catching up with him.

He shoved his duffel bag into my chest. "Do an old man a favor," he said.

I grabbed at the bag, but it skidded to the ground in front of me. I stumbled over it as he walked on. He headed through the kitchen and into the garage through a side door.

Slinging the duffel over my shoulder, I ran to catch up with him. For an old man with prostate cancer, he moved pretty well.

"I thought we were going to my place," I said.

"I need to get a few things first," he said.

He switched on the lights and rattled his key ring until he found the key he wanted. Moving to his gun cabinet, he opened the padlock and swung the doors wide.

"There's another duffel bag on the wall," he said. "Get it."

I grabbed where it hung on a nail hammered into one of the studs. He began pulling weapons out of the cabinet.

"Not this again," I said.

"Just shut up and give me the bag."

He unzipped it and laid it open on the table. Two AK-47s and fistfuls of clips went in, followed by a couple of pistols and more ammo.

"What are you doing, Seymour?"

"If you think I'm going out to your place unarmed, think again. If anyone shows up, I'm gonna be ready.

"C'mon," he said, walking back out the door, leaving the bag for me.

A duffel over each shoulder, I trotted again to catch up. He walked past the police cars blocking the drive, opened the passenger door of my car, and got in. I put the duffels on the back seat and climbed into the driver's side.

"Drive," he said, "before those government bastards change their minds about letting us go."

4

FUCKING Ingrams. That goddamn do-gooding family has been ruining life in Litchfield for a hundred and thirty years. You'd think I'd have known better than to have anything to do with them. But as always, they suck you in with their goddamn idealistic notions, their bogus nobility and chivalric posturing, and look what it leads to.

But there I was again sitting beside the youngest and possibly craziest Ingram in the history of this doomed clan, weapons in the back seat, danger lurking in the trees and behind the bushes, my only friend in this world murdered because of his last mad crusade, thoughts of revenge in mind, and damn me if I didn't feel better than I had in months. The pain in my spine had settled down to a dull roar, blood pounded in my neck, and I felt like I had a purpose again.

"Where do you want to go?" Nelson asked as he drove the old LTD down the back roads.

"Back to your place," I said.

I wanted to check out the terrain before dark. Whoever killed William would likely come gunning for Nelson next with my house all covered up with the police, and I aimed to catch the son-of-a-bitch. I pulled out the immediate-release morphine from my pocket, opened the vial, and downed a couple of the pills. It was going to be a long night and I had to stay limber.

"What are the pills?" Nelson asked, looking from me to the road.

"Grandpa's medicine," I said.

I AM a pathologist. I have spent the better part of forty years examining death. Hefting gobs of bloody tissue in my hands and peering through the microscope at slides, I parsed out the causes of death and predicted where death awaited the living. Sometimes I wasn't sure why I ever chose this line of work. After four years of medical school I hadn't much use for my fellow man. I had little patience for their hard luck stories and couldn't abide the unkempt spectacles they made of themselves in life. Illness brings out the worst in most people. A needy woman becomes whining and helpless. A domineering man wages war from his bed, fighting over every detail of his care. An old man thrown into a hospital bed, stripped of the reassuring pattern of his daily life, deprived of all the cues and touchstones that tie him to his reality, gives in to the senility that has stalked his days like a shadow and becomes a drooling, incontinent husk of himself. I couldn't stand the sight of it and hadn't the patience to cajole these unfortunate people back toward health.

At the time, I could not have put this in so many words. I only knew that I was put off by the hospital wards and drawn toward the cleanliness and order of the pathology labs. It is amazing to me how many of life's most important decisions are made instinctively, unreflectively, even casually. So, out of a need for order and repulsion for the mess of living and dying, I ended up a pathologist, and ironically dealt with the bloodiest messes of the living and the dead.

So be it. It suited my temperament. I was good at it. However, it did little to take the unformed homunculus that had emerged from eight years of college and medical school unscathed by any life experience and turn him into a human. For that particular, bittersweet redemption I had my wife to thank. We married at the end of my pathology residency. She had been a microbiology technician and we had met during a rotation I spent in that section of the lab. She saw something worthwhile in me, though I still don't know what. She took care of me, forced me to develop a circle of friends, bore me a son, taught me what happiness was about. And sadness. Over forty years of marriage she tried her hardest to make me into something resembling a human, and ironically, opened me up principally to life's boundless ability to inflict pain. We had a son only to lose him in Vietnam. Lacy died of metastatic breast cancer. I had to read out the slides and predict her death.

In the wake of her death, William and I had sat together in that big house like two castaways pretending we both had a reason to live. And now he was dead, too. So, after seventy-five years of intemperate and indifferent godlessness, occasional recklessness, and bouts of ego and self-delusion, here I was the only one left standing. And in the seat beside me sat the double-recessive final scion of the most doomstruck family in this county. I didn't give a goddamn whether I lived or died, and he couldn't find his way out of the bottle or the pall of his dead father, and between the two of us we were supposed to deal with mob hit men and God knows what other kinds of shitstorms heading our

way. It struck me as funny all of a sudden and I couldn't
help laughing out loud.

"What's so funny?" Nelson asked.

He eyeballed me, probably trying to decide if I'd gone
over the edge. The goddamn beautiful fall afternoon still
was all around, like God was laughing back at me. I
reached back and grabbed one of the 9mm's from the duffel bag and jacked a magazine into it.

"Nothing," I said. "Just get me to your place before
dark."

5

HARTLEY and I drove down the back roads toward the cabin. He was fuming and fiddling with one of his pistols, snapping a clip into it and jacking a round into the chamber.

"Just what did you have in mind with that?" I asked.

Satisfied with the gun, he set it in his lap and reached for another and loaded it.

"I'm going to catch the son-of-a-bitch," he said.

With both pistols in his lap, he reached now for the AK-47s and jacked clips into both of them.

"We've been down this road before," I said, "and it almost got us killed."

"Just drive," he said.

As I drove down the narrow track that led onto the Georgia-Pacific lot, Hartley looked around at the empty run of trees.

"Where's the damn cabin?" he asked.

"Over there," I said, pointing through the trees to my neighboring lot.

"Then why are we parking here?" he asked.

"I've been putting my car here," I said, "to kinda not declare too loudly that I'm at home. In case someone comes looking."

"But now we're trying to catch the bastards," he said. "We want them to know that you're home." He gestured toward the cabin. "Park it right out there in the open so they can see it."

Seeing he was in no mood to be argued with, I put the car in reverse and backed out of the lot. After a moment on the roadway again, I pulled down the drive to the cabin. The tree limbs had grown since I'd last driven down it and the branches brushed the windows and whipped my antenna around.

As I parked, Hartley climbed out and surveyed the lot dyspeptically.

"Keeping things up around here," he said, staring at the clutter in the yard.

"I like the rustic look," I replied, pulling the duffel bags out of the back seat.

"You mean the trailer-trash look," he said as he grabbed an AK-47 from the front seat and jammed a pistol into his belt. "Stow that stuff upstairs and then I want to walk the property line before it gets dark."

I scrambled up to the cabin and stashed the bags on the bed, then came back downstairs. Hartley stood down by the riverbank, staring at the Sour Mash as it flowed past.

"Any sign last night that they came from the water?" he asked as I came up beside him.

I shrugged. "Didn't hear any boats, but it was pretty stormy last night. They probably could have pulled up in a semi and I wouldn't have heard them."

He shot me a disgusted glance. "C'mon," he said and

began walking upriver along the bank. "May as well be doing this myself."

"Look, Seymour," I said, "I'm sorry William's dead, but I didn't kill him! I didn't ask you to get involved in this last year. Now, we're both in a world of trouble here, and walking around pissed at me isn't going to get us anywhere."

He turned and looked at me again, disgusted at first, but then he smiled crookedly. "Best thing I've heard out of you all day."

The day had matured into a lovely, dry autumn afternoon, the wind rippling through the leaves, a golden light in the air as the sun westered. The scent of wood smoke came to me as the people in the surrounding miles of forest lit up their fireplaces against the coming of the first cold night of the season.

"Nice afternoon," I said, walking beside Hartley, the rifle riding loose on my hip.

He snorted. "Don't believe it," he said. "Just one of God's tricks to lull you into a false sense of security."

We came to the fence line along the upriver end of the property. Hartley squatted alongside the ratty wire fence and sighted down its length. Then he stood and began slowly walking along.

"Just what are we looking for?" I asked.

He walked on, keeping his eyes on the fence and the ground alongside it. "Someone tried to come through your front door last night," he said. "If they come back, they're likely to come by the same route. So, if I find where they crossed onto to your property, then I've got a leg up in catching them."

He bent down and scrutinized the ground. "Rain last night washed most everything away," he said. He looked across the Georgia-Pacific property to the cabin on the next lot. Smoke rose gently from its chimney.

"Who lives there?" he asked.

"I don't know. I've seen one guy coming and going. Tall. Dark-skinned."

"What's he doing out here?"

"What is anyone doing out here? As little as possible. I've seen him fishing off the bank from time to time."

Hartley harrumphed and went back to inspecting the fence, following the line through the trees. We reached the far corner, where the property line turned to parallel the road. He stopped there, fingering the wire. Right at the corner, the top part of the wire was bent down and pushed in. The weeds that sat along the ground had been trampled down on both sides of the fence. Among the weeds lay a cigarette butt.

"It was here," he said. He turned and looked back to the house. "He came over the fence here, then crept through the trees along this side of the property until he was opposite the house."

He walked back, tracing the path he'd just described. Back down along the bank, he looked up at the cabin.

"You have any floodlights to light up the area around the house?" he asked.

"One," I said, pointing to the light tacked up beside the porch. "It shines where the car's parked."

"We'll have it on tonight," he said. "And the porch light. Hell, turn on all the damn lights."

We walked back to the house. Hartley looked along the river. Between the house and the river, the ground fell away, about a four-foot drop-off before you came to the water.

"I'll be down there," he said, "in the shadow of the house. If anyone comes up the stairs, I can slip in behind him without too much trouble."

"And what am I supposed to do?"

"You'll be up there. In the cabin being very obviously

and carelessly home. Turn the TV up loud and make sure
he can see you moving around inside."

"I don't have a TV."

"Well, the radio, then."

"So, I'm the bait?"

He looked at me. "You'll be armed. Probably better'n
him. Just try not to shoot him. It's hard to just wound a
man with an AK-47 and I want this bastard alive."

"This is really nuts," I said. "Shouldn't we just let the
Feds help us out here?"

"Shit, son," Hartley said, "don't start with that again.
Now why don't you go see what you've got for dinner
while I get ready for these bastards."

6

Hartley

D ARK found me hunkered down along the riverbank, peering out between the support poles of the cabin. The night had turned cold, and this skinny old man didn't have much protection against it. I huddled in my jacket and jammed a hand under either armpit. The ground here was still muddy from yesterday's rain. The best I could do was squat down on a tarp I'd laid out, tucked up against a rock.

Meanwhile, up in the cabin, Nelson was warm and cozy. I could hear the radio playing and his heavy footfalls across the thin flooring. The poor boy was nervous as a tick. He'd been up there by himself for almost two hours and had paced the whole time.

I sat there and thought of William Charles and Lacy and Alexander, my son, and of the stretch of years that separated me from anything like innocence. It seemed only yesterday that I had been twenty-four and full of promise, my whole life before me. How had it come to this, everything gone, everything contracted down to this muddy trench along this tired river, my whole life gone, to be spoken of now only in the past tense and with regret? The measure of one's age can be had from the ceremonies one attends and the tense of one's verbs. Childhood and young adulthood are all graduations and weddings and baptisms and the future tense. Old age is funerals and the past imperfect.

Out on the road the sound of an engine began to roll in from far off. After a moment, a pair of headlights could be seen blinking through the trees, the engine's drone growing louder. This was not how our culprit would approach, but I wanted to see if its lights illuminated anything else along the road that didn't belong there.

But instead of cruising past, this car slowed down as if looking for something, the engine's pitch deepening as the driver downshifted. I stood and watched more closely.

Damnit if the car didn't turn into Nelson's drive and start bumping slowly down the track toward the house.

I reached for the AK-47 and thumbed off the safety. Staying in the shadow of the house, I moved between the support beams and put myself in the lee of the tool shed that leaned against the far end of the cabin.

The headlights raked across the yard as the car bounced into the clearing around the cabin. As it pulled into the arc illuminated by the floodlight off the stairs, I could see that it was a new Mercedes. From it I could hear the boom and rumble of an impressive stereo.

I squatted down beside the shed, keeping the gun at the ready. The car rolled to a stop. The passenger door snapped open and the din from inside suddenly broadcast itself across the yard.

A young black woman climbed out of the car. She seemed familiar, though I couldn't place her. She stood looking around the yard, then up at the cabin.

The engine shut down, gratefully killing the music. The driver's door opened and a thin white man climbed out. He wore sunglasses despite that fact that it was night. Lank hair was pulled back in a ponytail. A black T-shirt that looked a size too small for him had CHURCH OF SCIENTOL-OGY emblazoned across its chest. He reached back into the car and pulled out a bottle of Evian water. He slammed the door and looked around.

"Fuckin' dump," he said evenly, taking a swig of the water. He had that flat, featureless accent that spoke of godforsaken places like California.

The woman closed the passenger door and walked out into the middle of the yard.

"Nelson Ingram!" she shouted up to the cabin, "you up there? Get your ass out here!"

The door to the cabin opened and I heard Nelson's foot-steps on the landing to the stairs.

"Latoya?" I heard him call down. "Is that you?"

"Damn straight, Mr. Reporter," she said. "I'm back for more trouble!"

Not knowing quite what was up with these two, I held back in the shadows, kneeling next to the shed.

I heard Nelson's footfalls coming down the steps.

"This place still looks like a cracker shack," the black woman said.

"That's because it is a cracker shack," Nelson said.

He stood in the yard now, looking from them out into the dark, probably wondering where I was. The three of them stood there awkwardly for a moment.

The woman nodded toward her companion. "Nelson, this is Benny," she said.

Benny took in Nelson from behind his shades. "Howdy," he said, keeping one hand jammed into a jeans pocket and the other worrying his bottle of Evian.

"We were in the area . . . visiting Reggie's mother," she

said. "I was telling Benny about you and I wanted to see if I could still find this place. Didn't really expect you to be here."

"Nice spot," Benny said. "There's a river out there, right?" he asked, gesturing out into the dark.

"Just down the bank," Nelson said, pointing out into the dark.

"Any development?" Benny asked.

Nelson looked at him, uncomprehending.

"Is anyone building out here?" Benny asked. "You know, with the waterfront property and all?"

"Building?" Nelson asked incredulously. He laughed. "No," he said. "There hasn't been much development out here for a long time."

Benny considered this. He walked to the bank. "Man, it's nice out here."

"Try it in August," Latoya said. "It's like the waiting room to Hell."

"Why don't y'all come on upstairs," Nelson said. "I think I got a few beers in the fridge."

"That'd be awesome," Benny said.

"Y'all go on up," Nelson said, pointing the way toward the steps. "I've got to check something down here and then I'll be right after you."

The two of them moved out of sight and I heard their footfalls on the stairs. After a moment, Nelson walked back toward the bank where I'd been set up. I doubled-back under the house, coming up from behind him as he stood looking around for me.

I rapped the barrel of the gun against a support beam and he jumped a foot in the air, stumbling down the bank as he tried to turn toward me.

"Christ," he said, scrabbling back up the bank.

I motioned for him to be quiet and follow me. We

walked to the far end underneath the house, as far away from the windows as we could get.

"Who the hell are these people?" I asked, whispering.

"The girl is that one from last year. The wife of the man who got lynched. The one we rescued from the warehouse."

That was where I'd seen her before. "And the man?"

"I don't know," he said.

"Well, he doesn't look like our mob hit man."

"Not unless L. Ron Hubbard works for them, too."

"I wouldn't rule that out," I said, "but you need to get rid of them."

"I'll give them a couple of beers. Why don't you come up? I'll introduce you."

I shook my head. "No, we don't know what they're up to and the less they know the better."

"Jeez, she's just a friend stopping by to visit. I don't get that every day here."

"Precisely. It seems a bit too damn coincidental that they stop by just as all shit breaks loose."

"So you're going to hide down here in the dark?"

"Get rid of them." My back was starting to hurt like a bitch and I was in no mood to listen to them party up there while I squatted down here.

"How? I've got to at least pretend to be hospitable."

"Get them out of here. Take them down the road for a drink then excuse yourself."

He nodded. "There's that little dive down the way."

"Go in separate cars. Have one quick one then tell them you've got to get to bed or something."

He nodded again. "That could work."

"Nelson!" the woman called from the upstairs landing. "Where the hell are you?"

"Get on it," I said. "Flash your headlights when you're coming down the drive so I'll know it's you."

"Okay," he said and turned toward the stairs.

7

Ingram

BENNY and Latoya had already gotten into what was left of my Budweiser.

"All we found was this shit to drink," Latoya said, draining her bottle.

She seemed very different compared to the angry angel I had known briefly last year. Then she had smoldered from behind high walls, occasionally lashing out like a snake from its coil. Now, she seemed shrill and barely under control.

"Sorry," I said, "I'm on a tight budget."

"A budget!" she said. "Yeah, I'll bet you're on a budget after the score you made last year."

Benny grinned. "Latoya told me about that. Awesome shit, dude."

"Yeah. Awesome shit. Listen, this beer sucks. Why don't we drive to the bar down the road?"

"I like this guy already," Benny said.

"Anything beats hanging around this place," Latoya said.

Benny had his keys out already. "Let's roll."

He led the way down the stairs.

"I'll drive," Benny said, standing by his Mercedes.

"I'll follow you in my car," I said.

"No, man," Benny said, looking at my heap. "I got German engineering, leather seats, surround stereo, industrial-strength air-conditioning. You gotta ride." He pulled open the passenger door, smiling.

Latoya was at my elbow, ushering me toward the door. "You gotta ride, Mr. Reporter."

The seats were black leather soft as a lover's bottom. Latoya slid into the back seat from the driver's side and Benny climbed behind the wheel.

"Fucking Nazis, man," he said, turning the keys in the ignition. "Really know how to build motor vehicles."

He put the car in reverse and gunned it backward, spinning rocks and dirt as he whipped the car around in an arc. Dropping it into first, he popped the clutch and headed down the drive.

"Which way?" he asked, crashing down the rutted dirt road.

"Right," I said. "It's down about a mile."

"Got it," he said. He turned hard when he hit the highway, tires squealing.

"Music!" Latoya shouted from the back.

He turned on the tape deck. Steely Dan boomed from the speakers.

Latoya leaned forward from the back seat. "Here, Mr. Reporter," she said. She handed me a joint.

"Light up," Benny said. He flicked a lighter to life in front of my face.

"Wow," I said, drawing at the joint as it flared to life. "It's been a while."

"Humboldt County," Benny said. "Really good shit."

I coughed at the first toke. Though I'd cut my teeth on various drugs back in the 1960s, I'd always been bored stupid by marijuana. Its effects were difficult to titrate and the potency of the stuff had increased tremendously since the middle seventies such that the highs had become unpleasantly intense and prolonged. Alcohol was much easier to manage and had the great advantage of being legal.

"Wow," I said again politely, passing the joint to Latoya.

She drew a prodigious toke and passed it on to Benny. He took it with one hand while he shifted into fifth gear with the other, steering with one leg tucked into the bottom of the wheel.

If I had stopped to think about it, taking the two of them to The Rebel Yell roadhouse was not the wisest of choices. It was a cinderblock building on a quarter-acre of asphalt that had served my needs for alcohol in the company of strangers on the odd times that I ventured out into the world from my river refuge. A neon Budweiser sign illuminated its only window. "Undistinguished" was the adjective that came to mind when one drove past, but more decisive words were elicited when one walked in the door. "Red Neck" were two of them.

A Rebel battle flag hung on the wall behind the bar. Cleavis, a skinny, bearded, lipless, chinless specimen of local inbreeding, stood wiping at the bar with a gray towel. The furnishings were otherwise sparse—Formica tables, tubular metal chairs, a few deer heads and racks of antlers on the walls. Good-ol'-boys of various ages were scattered through the room while Hank Williams, Sr., blasted from the jukebox. Photos of Donnie, Bobbie, and Davey Allison decorated the walls along with NASCAR memorobilia. In the past I had managed to blend in with the crowd by keeping my mouth shut and nodding sanguinely when topics like integration, welfare, or Communism came up. But now coming in with Latoya and Benny in tow, I was suddenly struck by what an imprudent decision coming here had been.

Cleavis eyed the three of us darkly as we entered. I'm not sure which was worse—Latoya's being black and stoned and sassy, or Benny's West Coast tea-shades, ponytail, and Scientology T-shirt. In any case, the welcome was lacking. Conversations stopped. Heads turned.

"Hey, Nelson," Cleavis said. "Y'all lost your way?"

"Hey, Cleave," I said. "Just stopping in for a drink with some friends from out West."

"Yeah?" Cleavis said skeptically.

"Hey, there," Benny said, stepping forward and holding out his hand. "Great place you got here."

Cleavis looked at the hand without moving.

"We'll just sit in the back," I said, pointing to the far corner. "If you could pull us a pitcher, I'll be back in a minute to get it."

Cleavis nodded without enthusiasm. Other people in the room followed us with their eyes.

"Goddamn," Latoya said, leaning into me, "think those boys in the back can play 'Dueling Banjos'?"

"Hush," I said, "They'll hear you."

"This place is awesome," Benny said, leaning in from the other side. "Really authentic."

"Yeah," Latoya said, whispering now, "authentic white trash."

"You are going to get us killed if you don't shut up," I said. I steered them to a table all the way in the back. I grabbed the chair up against the far wall with a view of the room, smiling and nodding at the good-ol'-boys who still eyed us coolly.

"Howdy," I said to the room in general. I motioned for

the other two to sit opposite me with their backs to the room so their voice wouldn't carry.

Cleavis held the pitcher of beer aloft at the bar, looking grimly in my direction. I went to get it. When I got to the bar, Cleavis drew the pitcher back and leaned forward.

"They ain't my usual *clientele*, Nelson," he said.

"Yeah, I know," I said. "We'll be quiet and leave after the pitcher."

"You got that right," he said, handing me the beer and the glasses.

Back at the table, I sat again and filled the glasses. "Let's drink up and then be on our way."

"I can't believe you're still living down here," Latoya said quietly. "After all the money you scored last year, I thought you'd be long gone."

I couldn't get over how different she seemed—effusive and barely in control, with hysteria lying just over the next hill.

"Yeah," Benny said, "'Toya here was telling me these wild stories about last year and I just said, like, 'No way, girl.' And she said, like, 'Way, white boy.' And she had to show me your place to, do her best to prove her bullshit story."

"I did more than prove my story," she said, "I produced the man."

"So what did she tell you?" I asked.

He rolled his eyes. "Some incredible story about the mob laundering money and her crazy brother trying to deal coke and getting her husband strung up by the mob and you stumbling into it and saving the day and stealing all the mob's money in the process."

I looked from him to her. "Well, that about covers it," I said, wishing she'd kept all that to herself.

"Jesus," Benny said, "how much did you score?"

I sipped at my beer. "Honestly, I don't remember."

"I'd guess a lot of money judging from the piece you gave to 'Toya."

"So, what brings you down this way?" I asked Latoya.

She looked down into her beer. "Visiting Reggie's mom. She hasn't seen Little Reggie since last year."

"And you, Benny?" I asked. "What brings you here?"

"Oh, man, I met 'Toya at community college. We were in the same sociology course. She said she was coming down South to visit and I jumped at the chance to come along."

"So you're a student?"

He fiddled with his beer. "I'm sort of a jack-of-all-trades. Sociology's one of my things."

"Really?" I said, topping off his glass. I was going to have to get this guy drunk to see what he was all about.

8

Hartley

I SAT out there in the cold awhile after they had left, but my back began to hurt like hell. When there was no sign of Nelson coming back, I stood up and walked the perimeter of his lot again.

There was nothing happening. I was tired. I was cold. My back hurt like a mother. I stood for a long while down by the drive looking out to the highway. No sign of Nelson.

I'd had enough. I stomped up the stairs to the cabin. The minimal warmth inside felt welcoming despite the shabbiness of the surroundings. I couldn't see how Nelson had put up with this place for the last year—cobwebs everywhere, dust a quarter-inch deep in the corners, a halo of dead mosquitoes and no-see-ums on the floor around all the lamps.

I slung my rifle onto the kitchen counter and went back to my bag, looking for my morphine tablets. I shook a cou-

ple of the immediate-release morphine pills out of the vial,
swallowed them dry, and stuffed the bottle into my pocket.
Back in the kitchen, I opened the last of Nelson's Bud-
weisers and chased the pills down.

Switching off all the lights, I stood out on the screened
porch. The river burbled past just a few feet out and twenty
feet down. The cold had stilled most of the insect life out
there and the night promised to be a quiet one.

How the hell did Nelson heat this place? As I recalled,
there was a way to shutter up these screens in the winter. I
looked around. An old wood stove sat in a corner.

He had a few sticks of fat pine for kindling lying beside
some small oak logs that looked like they were still a little
green. I crumbled up some newspaper into the stove, then
put in the kindling and lit things up. Once that had crackled to life, I fed in a couple of the logs, closed the grate,
and adjusted the vents.

I stood painfully, then limped to the overstuffed chair
nearest to the stove. Sitting there in the dark, I watched as
the light from inside the stove grew. The gnawing pain in
my back shrank slowly from the devouring of a mastiff
into the lazy chewing of an older hound dog, and from
there into the merely inconvenient nips of a lap dog as the
drugs took hold.

I must have dozed, for I found myself talking with
Lacy. She sat in a chair opposite me, bald as a billiard ball
from the chemo and thin as a stick. Smiling ruefully, she
asked me just what I thought I was doing.

"I got William murdered through my own careless-
ness," I said to her, "and I've got to make things right by
him."

She laughed at me. "You old fool! Just who do you
think you are—John Wayne?"

"No, Jimmy Stewart," I said, laughing with her.

"There's someone at the door," she said, pointing past my shoulder, still laughing.

And then she was gone. The room was dark except for the glow from the stove. I held a hand out to it, feeling the beginnings of the heat coming from it, missing her like a severed limb—a raw, painful absence. Her death had been agony for the both of us. I still couldn't bring myself to think of it. Without her I did indeed feel like a one-legged man, off-balance and about to fall. I didn't want to think about the past. It contained what had been the best of me and it was gone and I couldn't abide the ache and longing that it stirred up.

Then, beneath the crackling of the stove I heard a faint mechanical rattle out of place in the quiet.

I held my breath and listened closer.

The doorknob rattled again, then the door began to creak open slowly. I moved out of my chair and slid beside the kitchen counter, placing it between the door and me. My back and legs had stiffened and I moved like the old cancerous man that I was. I slid down onto the floor and yanked the 9mm from where I had jammed it into my pants.

The door swung wide open. I flicked off the safety. The floorboards creaked. I peered around the corner of the counter. A dark silhouette was framed in the dark doorway, too furtive and square and stocky to be Nelson. I took aim. I could have killed him where he stood, but I needed him alive to find out what he knew.

"Why don't you stop right there," I said.

The silhouette crouched down at the sound of my voice. I fired the 9mm, putting a round into the doorjamb beside him. Splinters flew and the whole house reverberated with the noise. He cringed away from the shot and I stood and moved forward, coming upon him as he staggered off to his left.

"Let's try it again," I said. "Just hold still and you won't get hurt."

His hand moved toward me. I fired a round into his thigh. He fell to the floor and the gun he had held skittered across the floor.

"Fuck!" he said in a nasal Midwestern accent.

I kicked the gun away and took a step back, switching on a lamp. He lay there sprawled on the floor, with a wild look in his eye.

"Move again and it'll be your nuts I shoot next," I said.

"Fuck you," he said.

I shot him in the other thigh. My ears were ringing and the smell of gunsmoke hung thick in the room.

"Goddamn, you!" he said. He was starting to bleed a fair amount.

"You think I'm kidding around?" I said. "You think you're the only one who knows how to kill things?"

"I'm gonna fucking kill you," he said.

"You wish." I pointed the pistol at his head. "Now get in that chair," I said, pointing at the chair beside him.

"You shot me in both my legs," he said. "How am I s'posed to fucking get up?"

"Figure it out," I said.

He looked from me to the chair, then started to crawl toward it. He pulled himself up into it, then turned and sat down painfully.

"Goddamn," he said, "who the fuck are you?"

"Someone you should have left alone," I said.

I walked behind him, closed the door, and grabbed a roll of duct tape off the kitchen counter where I'd left it earlier. I handed it to him, keeping the gun on him.

"Tape your right arm to the handle of the chair," I said.

He looked from the duct tape to me, judging his chances then snatched the roll reluctantly from me. Awkwardly he ran a couple of turns of tape around his arm.

When he was done, I reached down and tore the roll free. I circled behind him, peeling some more tape loose, and taped his free arm down. Last of all, I taped him firmly to the back of the chair, trusting that his gunshot legs would keep him from struggling too hard.

"You are making a mess of my wood floors," I said.

"Fuck you," he said, beginning to break into a sweat. "Just kill me and get it over with."

"You'd already be dead if that was my chief concern," I said, then walked into the bedroom. I retrieved my doctor's satchel, and went back out the main room. The adrenaline was starting to fade and my back began to ache with a hard, bony pain.

Pulling up a chair, I sat opposite him. I could see he, too, was in a lot of pain and trying hard not to show it. Blood soaked his trousers. He was a thickset man, no longer young, with thick black hair combed back in a pompadour, a Roman nose, and dark brown eyes squinting from behind heavy lids.

"So," I asked, "are you the son-of-a-bitch who broke into my house and killed my friend?"

"That old colored housekeeper?" he asked, smiling with a grimace. "He got in the way."

My heart pounded and the blood roared in my ears. I took a deep breath. "You've got two more extremities I can still put bullets in before I even start on any vital organs. You'd best mind your manners and tell me what I need to know."

"Fuck you, Granddad," he said and spat at my feet.

I pulled my Buck knife out of my pocket and opened the blade.

"You gonna cut me now, Granddad?"

I stood and cut the sleeve off his jacket and shirt with the knife, laying bare his arm. Then I went back into my satchel and retrieved the vials of lorazepam and morphine.

The morphine came already dissolved in a glass ampule
ready for a syringe, but the lorazepam was still a powder
in its little vial. I injected a couple of cc's of sterile saline
into the vial and shook it to dissolve the drug. All the
while, my guest sat in his chair, beginning to hyperventi-
late a little as the pain ate into him and his own supply of
adrenaline faded. He looked worriedly at the vials I was
preparing.

"What's that shit?" he asked.

"Medicine," I said.

These days it wasn't easy to come by such things, what
with Uncle Sam's obsession with controlling narcotics. In-
jectable drugs were monitored and left a paper trail that
was simple to track. But I had a few anesthesiologist
friends who had salted away modest amounts of these
drugs by overreporting what they used in the operating
room. Usually they'd have been reluctant to admit it, much
less part with any of their stash. But ever since I'd showed
up with metastatic prostate cancer, deep wells of sympathy
had opened up in the hearts of these aging colleagues. So,
in anticipation of ending my own life comfortably when
the pain became too much to bear, I'd accumulated a re-
spectable supply of drugs of recreation and abuse.

I wiped his arm clean with his shirtsleeve and injected
him first with 5 milligrams of morphine. Enough to take
the edge off his pain and lower his inhibitions. Then I gave
him 2 milligrams of the lorazepam. Giving it intramuscu-
larly was dodgy—the rate at which his body absorbed it
would be hard to predict—but it was the best that I could
do. In the old days they used scopolamine or Pentothal for
this purpose. You'd induce a twilight sleep and then you
could ask the person questions that they, in their half-
awake state, tended to answer truthfully.

As the morphine took hold, the furrows in his forehead
began to smooth out and his breathing eased.

"Fuck me. If this is torture, sign me up," he said.

I sat down opposite him again and lit a cigarette. He watched me hungrily.

"You got one for me?" he asked.

I shook loose a second one, put it in his mouth, and lit him up. He drew heavily at it.

"Excellent," he said. "Camels. Fuck that low-nicotine shit."

"Lung cancer's not my big worry," I said.

"Me neither right now."

We smoked together in silence. The ash from his cigarette grew long and finally fell onto his shirt. The only sound was the crackling from the wood stove. My back started to hurt in earnest and I seriously considered using the rest of the morphine for myself. But I had to stay sharp. His eyes had drifted shut, and the cigarette dangled from his lips, smoldering. Just before it fell to his shirt, I took it from him. I stubbed both our smokes out on the floor.

Pulling my chair closer to him, I asked him in a low voice:

"You still with me, buddy?"

His eyes fluttered, drifted open, then closed again. "Yeah, I'm here."

"What's your name?"

He stirred again. "Eddie . . ." he said distantly.

"Nice to meet you, Eddie," I said.

"Sure," he said.

"Listen, Eddie, was that you that broke into my house and killed my friend?"

He breathed evenly. "Yeah."

"What were you looking for?"

He began to snore. I nudged him a bit near one of his leg wounds. The pain brought him up to a lighter place in his sleep. "What were you looking for in my house, Eddie?" I asked again.

"Old man. Hartley."

"Why?"

"Payback," he said.

"On whose orders?"

This was harder for him. His eyes opened. He looked cross-eyed at me.

"Clip the old man. Big Frank."

"Who's Big Frank?"

"Big Frank Losurdo," he said lazily.

"Where is he from?"

"Tampa."

"Who's he with in Tampa?"

"Trafficante."

"Is he a crime boss?"

"Clip the old man and bring in Ingram," he said.

"You wanted Ingram for payback?"

"Alive."

"Why did you want him alive?"

His eyes fluttered. "See what he knew."

"About what?"

"See what he knew."

"About what?"

He sank deeper under the lorazepam, snoring again. I prodded him. He stirred a little but didn't answer.

"Eddie," I said loudly.

He groaned and coughed.

From my left, heavy footfalls came up the steps. I stood and grabbed the 9mm off the kitchen counter. The front door flew open and two men came through. I crouched and ran.

The flat reports of machine pistols filled the room as their guns fired a spray of rounds. I kept moving, the shots following my steps, embedding themselves into the flooring. Splinters flew up. Smoke billowed from the muzzles.

I rolled onto the screen porch. Hitting the floor took my

wind away, the pain in my back shooting all the way to my heels. The spray of bullets passed over my head. There was nowhere to go. In a second they'd be on me.

I looked onto the porch out toward the river. There was nowhere else to go. Forcing myself to my feet, I pushed off from the floor and through the screening on the edge of the porch. Thirty years old and corroded almost clean through, it gave way easily and I was free into the dark and falling.

Twenty feet down. I prayed my momentum would carry me clear of the bank and into the river. I could see nothing. The staccato reports of the guns chattered behind me. I took one breath of icy air as I fell.

Water hit my face and chest while my knees came up against something harder. Pain was everywhere. I tried to breathe but took in a mouthful of water.

I coughed and tried to push off from the bank, getting my head above water and pulling at the air. After a moment, I was able to kick out free from the bank. I was adrift in the river now, but could see nothing. I breathed water again, then air, floundering.

There was no bottom to the pain in my back and legs. It was the only thing left in the universe. Rolling onto my back, I let the river take me.

BOOK 2

Evil is unspectacular and always human,
And shares our bed and eats at our own table.

—W. H. Auden

9

WELL past midnight, Benny drove back to the cabin, sliding the Mercedes through the turns. Drunk after too many pitchers of beer, I held on to the armrest and tried not to throw up as he lurched down the road.

"That place was too much," Latoya hooted from the backseat.

"Very authentic," Benny said.

"Yeah, it was real authentic when that big cracker came to our table and asked you to go outside with him," she said to him.

"I guess I shouldn't have insulted Hank Williams, Jr.," Benny said.

He pulled the car through another turn, pressing me into the door.

We should have left after the first pitcher when whatever passed for Southern civility in the bar was still in effect. But we had a second and then a third pitcher, which

Cleavis reluctantly drew for us, his anger stoking slowly.
Then Hank, Jr., had come on the jukebox and Benny felt
compelled to give voice to his opinions on the subject loud
enough to carry throughout the room. I think the precise
term he used for Hank was 'mutant cracker asshole.'

Unfortunately, several of the patrons at nearby tables
were long-standing Hank fans. Clint McConneyhead, a
Vietnam vet still clanging from the bell ringing he'd gotten there, pulled all six feet six inches of his wiry self up
out of his chair, closed the space between us in two strides,
scraggly hair and scraggly beard framing his wild eyes that
still saw Charlie behind half the bushes.

"What did you say, son?" he asked, leaning far down
into Benny's face.

Benny seemed clueless as to the peril he was in. He
smiled at Clint and repeated his comment about the Son of
the King of Country.

Clint nodded. "That's what I thought you said." His
eyes narrowed and he drew in air heavily through his nose.
He hovered over Benny, looming like bad weather.

"Take it back," he said.

"Excuse me?" Benny asked, still smiling obliviously.

"Take it back," Clint said. "Take back what you said."

His nostrils flared, he chugged air like a locomotive.
Clint and I had shared a few beers on more than one occasion, and while generally a retiring, soft-spoken fellow, he
felt passionately about a few things, the legacy of the
Williams family being one of them.

Benny stared at him, a look of puzzlement beginning to
cloud his face. He looked over at me.

"Apologize to the man, Benny," I said.

"I was just kidding around," Benny said.

Clint had him by the collar and hauled him up out of his
chair before he knew what was happening.

"Jeez," Benny said, "I'm sorry. I was just kidding. Hank's cool."

"He's a goddamn prince," Clint said.

"Sure," Benny said.

"Say it!" Clint said, shaking him like a rag doll.

"He's a goddamn prince," Benny said, pale and trembling, vainly trying to pull Clint's hands loose from his collar.

"Damn straight he is," Clint said. He let go of Benny, who settled heavily back into his chair. "Now y'all best leave," he said.

"Now wait just a damn minute," Latoya began, but before she could go on, I had her by the hand and headed toward the door.

"Not now. Not here," I said. "Let's move it, Benny."

Out in the parking lot, I moved them rapidly to the car, hoping no one would follow.

"Wow," Benny said, "he was really pissed off."

"Yeah," I said. "He really likes Hank, Jr. The last time I saw him this mad, he hauled a man outside and beat him stupid over a disagreement about Waylon Jennings."

"Cracker son-of-a-bitch," Latoya said, spitting onto the gravel.

"Well, that *was* my neighborhood bar," I said regretfully as I climbed into the car.

"Fuck 'em," Latoya said, climbing in the back seat behind Benny.

Benny started the car and peeled out of the parking lot. "Man," he said, shaking his head.

A S we rounded the last few turns on the way back to the cabin, I saw an orange glow from the woods ahead. I leaned forward, to try to see where it came from.

Benny pulled the car into the drive and the orange glow filled the woods in front of us.

"What the hell . . ." Benny said.

The cabin was ablaze. Benny pulled the car to a stop on the edge of the clearing. I stood beside the car. It was all gone, the whole thing on fire, flames up into the trees.

Latoya was at my side.

"Goddamn," she said.

I ran forward. "Seymour!" I shouted. "Seymour!"

The heat of the fire stopped me from coming closer. I peered into the flames, but could see little.

"Dr. Hartley!" I shouted, but the only reply was the crackling of the flames.

Half the house came crashing to the ground and settled among the burning pilings, sending up a cloud of smoke and ashes.

Benny came up beside me. "There's nothing left in there, man," he said. "You'd better back off before you get hurt."

"What if he's still in there?"

"Who?" Benny asked.

"Dr. Hartley. He was staying with me."

"I'd say he's toast if he's in there, man."

A car rounded the curve out on the road, slowed, and turned in the drive, headlights bouncing as it rolled toward us. A sheriff's patrol car. After a moment, a deputy climbed out and came toward us. Since the events of last year, a lot of the sheriff's department staff had turned over and I didn't know him.

"You all live here?" he asked.

I nodded. "I do."

"I called the fire department," he said, " but they'll be a while getting out here. Probably too late to save anything."

"There was someone staying with me," I said. "I just hope he wasn't in there."

"Any idea what happened?" he asked.

I shrugged. "There's a propane tank under the house. I guess it could have sprung a leak . . ."

Just then, something underneath the house exploded and a huge fireball blossomed outward from the flames.

"Holy shit," I said. We all turned and ran back toward the cars.

The heat came first as if we had passed inside an oven. Fire rolled toward us, hugging the ground and rippling into the sky. As we made the trees and dove behind the Mercedes, the wave of flames thinned and slowed, ascending into the air. In another second it had passed, though the cabin now burned even more wildly.

"I think that was your propane tank," the deputy said, still peering out from where we all squatted in the lee of the car.

"Good thing it was almost empty," I said.

"Man," Benny said, "I think I pissed myself."

Latoya sat on the ground, leaning against the back bumper of the car. "Goddamn, Ingram. You gotta be on Trouble's A-list."

We huddled there for a long while watching things burn. My home and all that I owned was gone. My father's shotgun, all my papers, everything. Strangely, it wasn't such a bad feeling. Except for worrying about Hartley, I wasn't unhappy to see it all go. I felt suddenly lighter, as if I had just been relieved of a weight I hadn't even known I'd been carrying.

After about half an hour the volunteer fire truck rolled in, but things were pretty much over by then. We pulled our cars out of the way and they drove their truck by and hosed down what was left. I sat against the front bumper of the Mercedes and watched while Benny and Latoya huddled inside the car against the cold.

When the firemen had finished, the cabin was just a

smoking ruin, cinders and ash and burnt boards lying among the pilings. I walked up and peered into it, the deputy beside me shining a flashlight into the rubble. The stove, fridge, and sinks lay in a pile in the center of the heap. I could make out the metal frames and wire springs from the beds. My car, parked beside the cabin when it went up, had a cracked windshield, burnt paint, and the tires looked a little melted.

"Don't see no bodies," the deputy said, "but we're gonna have to sift through things."

I waded in carefully among the wreckage and began to poke around. Everything gone. Maybe this would be enough to finally bury my father's ghost.

Another pair of headlights rolled down the drive and into the clearing. I turned to see who it was. A tall man climbed out of the car with a tired but business-like gait, backlit by the headlights. As he came closer, I could see that it was Jack Edmonds, dressed still in his dark suit despite the late hour, his necktie still knotted tight.

He stood at the edge of the remains of the cabin and shook his head. "I can't leave you alone for a minute, Ingram."

He turned to the deputy. "What do we know?"

The deputy looked around at the smoking remains of the house. "The cabin burned down."

Jack looked down at his feet and shuffled them a bit in the dirt. "Yes, deputy," he said patiently, "I can see that."

"I don't know what happened," I said. "Hartley came to stay with me for the night, but some friends dropped by. We went out for a few drinks and left him here. When we came back. . . ."

Edmonds looked around. "Friends?"

"Over there," I said, pointing toward the Mercedes.

Edmonds nodded. "I noticed the high-priced ride," he

said. "California plates. Very out of place. How about some introductions?"

"Sure."

We walked together toward the car, and I motioned for Latoya and Benny to come out. After a moment, the driver's door snapped open. Benny leaned his head out.

"Benny," I said, "I'd like you to meet someone."

Reluctantly, he stood. "Howdy," he said, standing protectively behind the open door of the car.

"Benny, this is an old friend of mine, Jack Edmonds. He's with the FBI."

Benny smiled. "Awesome," he said, reaching out a hand.

Jack returned an unenthusiastic handshake. "You're a long way from home."

"Just visiting," he said.

"So, how do you know Nelson?"

"Latoya here knows him." Benny nodded to Latoya as she sat in the passenger seat.

"Latoya Copley?" he asked. "The wife of the Reginald Copley?" He leaned over and peered into the darkened window.

She opened her door and climbed out.

"Mrs. Copley," he said, "what brings you back this way?"

"Family business," she said, suddenly hooded and smoldering again.

Edmonds motioned to the deputy. "Get statements from these two, Officer," he said.

The deputy fumbled for his notepad. "You first, sir," he said, nodding at Benny. "In the patrol car, please."

Benny threw up his hands. "Man, I'm just a tourist here."

"This is bullshit," Latoya muttered.

Jack took me by the arm and led me back toward the remains of the cabin. "Hartley left his house on a tear this afternoon. Just what were you trying to do out here?"

I stared again at the wreckage. "He was trying to catch the son-of-a-bitch. He figured he would come back tonight looking for me."

"And you went out for drinks and left him here alone?"

"I didn't think anything would happen."

He grabbed me by the shoulder and turned me to face him.

"Nelson," he said, "let's cut the crap. I don't know what the hell went on at those warehouses last year, but it seemed that there was more than you were letting on. I thought we'd just let sleeping dogs lie, but now all this bullshit breaks loose, your house burns down, Hartley disappears, and this Copley woman blows in from L.A. in a forty-thousand-dollar car with Don Johnson at the wheel, and you want me to believe it's all just a coincidence?"

"Listen, I was just laying low trying not to be noticed. Why don't *you* tell me what's going on here?"

"Do you know just what you ran into last year?" he asked.

I shrugged. "Drugs. Money. Guns."

Jack shook his head. "That was just the tip of the iceberg. That bust set off a shit storm on both sides of the law."

"What do you mean?"

"You stumbled into a money-laundering scheme for a big chunk of the drug trafficking for the Northeast and South. We seized well over ten million in cash. That embarrassed a lot of people, but you don't know the half of it.

"Since the early days, the *Cosa Nostra* has had a policy not to get involved with drug trafficking. It's a federal rap, and they wanted to steer clear of the Feds whenever possible. But there's so much money in it, these guys can't stay away from it. When crack came to this country, they made so much money, they didn't know what to do with all the cash. They couldn't use their usual channels for money laundering, because officially they weren't dealing drugs at all and the higher-ups didn't want to know about it. And when you got them busted, not only were they out a huge chunk of change, but they also had a lot of explaining to do to the bosses who thought they'd never gotten their full taste of the action."

He turned to face me. "So there's more than a few people who'd leap at the chance to serve up a little payback. Obviously, someone's found out about your role in last year's arrests. Probably from the late Sheriff Stanton. There's a contract out of Tampa. We don't know who. But the word is that they're looking for something more than just your ass."

"Like what?"

"Why don't you tell me?"

I stared at him in the dark. "I don't know, Jack."

"Listen, Nelson," he said, "I don't know if you're protecting someone or you just don't understand what this is all about. These people are trying to kill you. Or worse. I can't help you if you shut me out."

He had a point. But there was too much explaining to do and I didn't think I could open up to him without putting Latoya at risk as well. But then there was Hartley to think about, too. I needed to find him, and Jack could be of help to me there. I looked over to the Mercedes. Latoya glowered at us. I looked back at Jack.

"I took some money," I said. "From the warehouses. But I gave most of it away."

"I'd figured that much out already," he said. "Never thought it was worth pursuing. But if it was just payback for some stolen money, I think you and Hartley would already be dead. Was there anything else?"

I thought for a moment. "I took a notebook and some computer disks."

"What was in them?"

"I never looked at the computer disks. The notebook had a lot of figures. Numbers, like a ledger."

"Why'd ya take them?" he asked. "You know you could have impeded our investigation."

I shrugged. "I don't know. I thought I might need an edge someday and they looked important. Maybe it was a mistake, but once I had them I would have had to admit too much to turn them over."

He leaned in close to me. "Where are they? They weren't in the cabin, were they?"

"They're safe," I said. I still didn't want to give everything up to him. I needed a few bargaining chips.

"I need to know where they are."

"They're safe," I said. I looked over at the cars. The deputy was trying to interview Latoya, but she stood there hanging fire and spitting out one-word answers.

"Why don't we talk in the afternoon at the police department," I said. I needed some time to think what to do next. "I'll tell you all about it then."

He started to argue with me again, but I stopped him. "Look, Jack, I'm drunk, I'm tired, my house just burned down, Hartley's missing. Let me catch a ride into town to sleep this off and I'll meet you in the afternoon and I'll bring the stuff. I promise."

"You're gonna stay with your uncle in Litchfield?"

"Sure," I said.

He nodded. "Noon at the Litchfield P.D."

"I'll be there. You gonna sweep the area looking for Hartley?"

He cast around, looking out into the dark. "Not much to do until daylight. I guess I could get the sheriff knocking on the doors of the cabins around here."

Latoya shook her head and turned away from the deputy, who was still trying vainly to interview her. "I shoulda known better than to come anywhere near you again, Mr. Reporter," she huffed.

"Sorry," I said. "Could you give me a lift into town?"

"I would if Barney Fife here would get off my case," she said.

I turned to Jack.

"Okay, Deputy," he said, "Let's call it a night and let these people go."

"Excellent," Benny said, climbing back into the Mercedes. "Let's roll."

10

NO sooner had we pulled away than Latoya was laying into me. "Jesus, not only do you attract the sheriff, you bring in the goddamn FBI!"

"And you show up and my goddamn house burns down," I said.

Benny kept his eyes straight ahead, keeping to the speed limit as he steered down the country roads.

"Just what did you say to that guy?" he asked, upshifting.

"What do you mean?" I asked.

"What did you say to the fucking Fed?" he asked.

"Why the hell do you care?" I asked.

He pulled the car suddenly to the left onto a dirt road, throwing me against the passenger door. Slamming the brakes, he came to a stop and I was pitched forward into the dash. Before I could move, he was on top of me, something cold and metallic jammed into my neck.

"What the fuck did you tell the Fed?" Benny said evenly.

"Goddamnit!" I said, struggling.

He pressed me hard into the door.

"Tell him what he wants to know," Latoya cried. I could hear fear in her voice.

He threw me back into my seat and waved a 9mm in my face.

"Listen," Benny said, "I've had enough of this bullshit. Now I want to know what you told the Fed and what you know about what went down here last year."

"Who are you?" I asked.

"Do what he says," Latoya said in a high, tight voice. "You don't want to know who he is."

He smiled. "That's right."

I looked from him to Latoya. Her eyes were wide, his were masked behind his shades.

Was this more of their bullshit? "What do you want?" I asked.

"Man," Benny said, "it's like you're trying to piss me off."

"He wants to know what you told the cops," Latoya said.

"Fuck you both," I said. "You think I give a shit if you shoot me?" I was getting tired of all this.

"Suit yourself," Benny said, pointing the pistol at my chest.

"They've got Little Reggie!" Latoya shouted, reaching forward and pulling the pistol away. Benny snatched it away from her and cracked her across the face with his free hand.

"Fuck!" Benny said. "Do that again and you'll never see the little prick again."

"What?" I said, looking from Benny to her.

She lay huddled in the backseat, blood pouring from a

split lip. "They've got Little Reggie," she said. "They found me in L.A. They were gonna hurt him if I didn't lead them to you. Just tell them what they want to know."

"And just who the hell are *they*?" I asked.

"I don't believe this," Benny said. "Has anyone noticed that I'm the one holding the gun here? I ask the questions. You answer." He pointed the gun back at my chest.

I looked at the gun, then at Latoya. Her eyes were large and pleading.

"I told Edmonds about the money," I said. "About the money I took last year."

"What did you tell him about the money?" Benny asked.

"That I took it. I don't have that much of it. I gave most of it away."

He looked at me. I tried to meet his gaze directly.

"What else?" Benny asked, still not taking his eyes off me.

"Nothing," I said.

"Bullshit," he said. "There was something else."

I didn't answer.

"Where is it?" he asked.

"It was in the cabin," I said. "It's gone."

"Oh, God," Latoya said.

He shook his head. "You better hope you're lying," he said, pointing the gun toward Latoya in the backseat.

I looked at him. He raised his sunglasses and met my eyes. They were small, flat, emotionless eyes. Stone dead eyes worse than anything I'd seen in the mobsters last year.

"I've got it in a safe-deposit box," I said at last. "In town."

He smiled and patted me on the cheek. "That's better, cowboy," he said, putting the gun back in his lap. "You're gonna take us there in the morning, aren't you now?"

I nodded.

"Now I want you to drive so I can keep an eye on you."
He opened his door and climbed out.

I slid over into the driver's seat, my hands beginning to
tremble. Benny tramped around the car and slid into the
passenger seat. He took one look at me shaking behind the
wheel and started laughing.

"Look at the big reporter," he said. "Rattle your cage,
did I?"

He sat back in the seat and slid his shades back down
over his eyes. "Drive us into town," he said. "We'll camp
out at the motel until the bank opens."

"I thought you were staying with Latoya's mother-in-
law," I said.

"Yeah, right. Just drive," he said.

WE pulled into the Knight's Inn down along the Interstate. Across the street sat the town's McDonald's
and an all-night minute mart. It must have been four in the
morning and the air hung still and cold, the roads empty.

Benny walked up beside me. "How do you stand living
in this goddamn one-horse town?" he asked.

"Because exciting folks like y'all keep on comin' to
visit," I drawled.

"Who woulda thunk it," he said. "Such a big party in
such a little place." He nudged me. "Let's get inside."

Leading the way, he pulled a key from his pocket and
opened the door to a room on the lower level of the motel.
Latoya followed us.

It was a plain room smelling of cigarettes, with two
double beds and a television. Benny threw himself onto the
near bed, kicking back against the headboard. He grabbed
the remote control for the TV and switched it on.

Latoya drifted into the room. She settled uneasily in a
chair by the window, nursing her split lip.

"Shut the fucking door," Benny said as he began flipping through the channels.

I came inside and closed the door behind me.

"Cool," Benny said, staring at the tube, "It's *The Jeffersons*." He pulled the pistol out from his pants and lay it across his lap, then cranked up the volume on the TV.

"Sit down, Gomer," he said to me. "George and Weezie are on."

I went to the bathroom and dampened a washcloth in the sink, then came back and sat beside Latoya and dabbed at her lip. She took the towel from me and held it to her face.

"You okay?" I asked.

She nodded.

"She's fine," Benny said. "You shoulda seen the way I had to cuff her around to get her this far."

"Fuck you," she said evenly.

"Just who the hell are you?" I asked.

He picked up the gun and fiddled with it. "You don't want to know who I am."

The hours passed slowly. Benny flipped through the channels and provided commentary on the waste that filled the airways through these dead early morning hours. I lay down on the other bed and tried to sleep. Before I knew it, Latoya was lying beside me. I lay turned away from her, my face crushed into a pillow but watching Benny through half closed eyes.

Finally, Benny's lids drifted down, his grip loosened on the remote control, his breathing slowed. He began to snore. I calculated the distance between us. I could rise and close it in a step and have the gun in my hand.

Suddenly I heard Latoya whispering in my ear as she lay behind me, her head beside mine.

"I'm sorry to get you involved in this," she said in the quietest hiss.

I moved my head slightly to signal that I had heard her.

"He's crazy," she went on.

I turned my head to look at her. Brown almond eyes penetrating me, full lips glistening, walnut skin.

"I need your help," she went on. "Give him what he wants and he'll spare Little Reggie."

I met her eyes. How could I say no to that gaze?

I nodded and took her hand.

I turned to look at Benny. The gun lay unchaperoned in his lap.

She squeezed my hand harder. "Please. We need to play along," she said.

"Okay," I said.

I lay there in the motel room, watching Benny. The hard-washed cotton sheets, saggy mattress, and creaky bedsprings summoned up again the memory of my father and that trip to Washington. It was as if the aura of it had been hanging over this day, coloring it with presentiments of doom, so that none of the events today bore any real surprise for me. After half a day on the road we had checked into a Travelodge along the Interstate somewhere in north Georgia. All day he'd been grim but sober behind the wheel, but now in the room he brought a bottle of bourbon from his suitcase and sent me to get ice from the machine down the corridor. Then he settled back in his bed and began working at the bottle. We watched *Gunsmoke* reruns on the television, with a baggy Marshal Dillon and a sagging Miss Kitty making their way through the plot. Something about rustlers, as I remembered.

After he'd gotten a few drinks into the bourbon, his tongue loosened a little. He began offering commentary on the TV show. For the last couple of years it had been harder and harder for us to speak about anything beyond the most superficial things. At the time, I wouldn't have been able to identify a reason for this, but now in retro-

spect I could see that the dissatisfactions in his life had
been multiplying—his marriage, his law practice, the in-
equities of the time and place, the confines of thought and
opportunity. The choices he had made, each reasonable at
the time, had conspired finally to trap him.

Marshal Dillon was cut off in a box canyon and the
rustlers were closing on him, creeping from rock to rock.
They traded shots back and forth, ricochets singing all
around the marshal. Festus had ridden into town for help,
but it was doubtful he would return in time.

Unexpectedly, my father leaned forward and thundered
at the television, "Goddamnit! Don't just sit there and let
them box you in! Shoot the sons-of-bitches! You're Matt
Dillon! Shoot the bastards!"

His eyes were red with drink, his nostrils flared. He
pulled at his drink and pursed his lips as he watched the
screen.

"Festus ain't coming," he said.

I hadn't understood his vehemence and was glad once
he dropped off to sleep. I changed channels until I found
Lost in Space and watched the Robinson family find their
way through the cosmos. I longed to be Will Robinson,
precocious and invulnerable with a wise father and doting
mother. The night had seemed endless then as it was now.

11

Hartley

THE pain in my back roared. I lay somewhere in the dark in its thrall, trying to lie stock still in the hopes that this would help. Only gradually did I notice the dry, warm sheets and blankets that covered me. Only by degrees did the unfamiliar surroundings register—the old lath and plaster walls gray in the almost complete darkness, the musty scent of mildew accented with a heavy bouquet of tobacco.

How had I come here? I breathed hard with the pain and tried to remember.

I had fallen in the water and the river had taken me. I remembered floundering, trying to breathe and taking in water, then thrashing higher and getting some air, then back down and into the current, passing an eternity this way, wondering how long this would take before I would finally die. Then my knees and belly came upon something hard.

I found myself beached upon some rocks, slick with algae. I grabbed on to them, gasping and coughing. Reaching higher, my hands found branches. I pulled myself up and settled into a muddy bank. I tried to stand, but my legs gave way and I fell back into the water, crying aloud. The water of the river swirled around my chest and face. I thought I would slip back into the flow and give myself up to it. Then a shadow loomed above me from on the bank.

Strong hands pulled me clear of the water, sat me up, then hoisted me into the air. I settled across a strong shoulder and was borne up and away like a bag of feed. The pain in my back and legs was horrific. I cried aloud again, but gave myself over to this bearer.

"Quiet," I heard a man's voice speak to me, "you are safe now." He carried me through woods and I lost track of time, aware only of the pain.

NOW I found myself cleaned-up and bedded in this warm and homely place, dry and tidy but still in tremendous pain. There was a window to my right. Still dark outside. How long had I been here? I rolled to my side with the thought that I might get up, but that single move alone was enough to make me cry out again.

A shaft of light opened up in the far wall and widened as a door opened. A silhouette stood in the doorway and moved into the room. A man, tall, but moving compactly and quietly. He leaned over me and the heavy aroma of tobacco came off him.

"Awake?" he asked in an accent that suggested Hispanic places.

"Where am I?" I asked, gritting my teeth with the pain.

He held some pills to my lips. "Take these," he said.

I took them into my mouth. They had a familiar taste. "Morphine?" I asked.

"I found them in your pocket," he said. He brought a glass of water to my lips.

I pulled myself up on one elbow and took the glass from him, sipping enough to wash the medicine down. Illuminated by the light from outside, he looked tan with a heavy mustache beneath a Roman nose, a bald head glistening.

"Who are you?" I asked.

I could see him smile. "Do not question fate," he said. He covered me up and left the room, closing the door behind him. I was in darkness again.

I waited, feeling the warmth of the morphine fill me slowly. After maybe half an hour I rolled to my side again. It hurt like hell but I could bear it. I took a breath, dropped my legs over the side of the bed, and levered myself into a sitting position. Again the pain roared but subsided. The blood drained from my head and the dark room faded to black. I dropped my head into my hands and fought to keep from passing out.

After a second my head cleared again. What was I wearing? A terry-cloth bathrobe. And where was I? Rough plank floors, rafters exposed in a slanting ceiling, throughout the smell of damp and mold. I stood with difficulty, pausing for a second to get my balance, then headed for the door.

I pushed it open and squinted at the sudden glare of light from the room beyond. He was sitting in a rocker beside a lamp, a book in his lap, looking up at me, a cigar smoldering in his hand.

"You are up," he said, surprised. He was dark but not black. His features suggested someone of Arab extraction, but his accent was Latino. Gray hair flanked his bald dome, a thick mustache flecked with gray. His features were weathered and somewhere on the high side of sixty.

"Where am I?" I asked. "And who are you?"

He looked up at me. "I am the man who plucked you

from the rocks, carried you here, cleaned you up, and whose hospitality you now enjoy," he said evenly. "Who are you?"

He had a patrician crust to him that set me back. "I'm Seymour Hartley," I said.

"I apologize for the bathrobe," he said. "Your clothes were wet and caked with mud. I washed them out and they're drying on the porch."

I stood in the open doorway, casting my eyes about the main room of a cabin, plain furniture, bare walls.

"Please," he said, gesturing toward a chair across from him. "Sit. You must be very uncomfortable."

I took a step into the room, then another. He stood and pulled the chair closer for me. Grabbing on to its arms, I sat gratefully, letting go a breath as the pain eased off.

"So," he began, settling back in his rocker and regarding me, "how did you come to get into the river and wash up on my bank in the dead of night?"

I considered the question. "It's a long story," I said finally.

"I have time," he said, smiling.

"You haven't really answered my questions," I said. "Where am I and who are you?"

"You are in a cabin on the Sour Mash River," he said. "And I"—he hesitated, —"am an old man eking out his retirement here."

"I don't think that's an Alabama accent I'm hearing," I said.

"Are you from the cabin that's burning upriver?"

"What?"

"The one that all the gunfire was coming from?"

I stood, straightened up with difficulty, and moved to the window. He stood beside me and opened the door beside the window.

"You have to go out on the porch to see it," he said.

I followed him outside and onto the porch. The cold air swirled around me, cutting through the thin bathrobe. I pulled it more tightly around me.

"This way," he said, leading me to one corner of the porch, "through the woods."

The smell of smoke and burnt tar hung in the air. Through the trees I could see only a haze.

"Started just after I fished you from the river," he said. "The gunfire was before that. It's what got me out on the porch in the first place. Then I heard you wash up on my bank."

"I was at a friend's house," I said. "It's a very long story." I shivered in the cold and thought of Nelson, wondering if he'd gone up in that blaze, if the gunman I'd shot had perished in it, or if he and his accomplices had set it. They could be in the woods looking for me now.

"Let's get inside," I said, walking past him to the door.

Back inside, we sat again.

"The police were out there until about an hour ago," he said. "They'll probably come knocking on doors in the morning. What would you like me to tell them?"

"Who are you?" I asked.

"A man who has been around enough to know that the police are not always our friends."

I looked at him squarely. The police were not going to help me find the men who killed William and would only get in my way, but I had no idea what this man's angle was and what he was doing out here in these backwoods.

"The enemy of your enemy is your friend," he said.

"And you are my friend?"

"I know something about you," he said.

"Really."

"I know that you came from that cabin but that you did not live there," he said. "You do not wish to become involved with the police. You are old and ill, but you burn with a desire for something that drives you on and sends you running from the law. Something very personal."

He laughed and lifted a drink from the table beside him, sipping at what looked like whiskey. He saw that I was watching him.

"Would you like a drink?" he asked, rising.

Before I could answer, he'd moved to his little kitchen and poured me a tumbler, fishing some ice cubes from his freezer, and following them with a dollop of sugar.

I accepted the glass hungrily, holding it to my nose and inhaling the heady fumes. Rum. Drawing at it, savoring the hot bite of it, I still watched him the whole while. All of his movements were measured and precise. His eyes were sharp and missed nothing.

He spoke again. "I know that you came from that cabin because when gunfire erupts in the dead of night and an old man washes up on my bank, Ockham's Razor dictates that the two events are connected. I know that you do not live there, because I have seen who lives there—a younger man who has lived alone for as long as I've been here. I know that you do not wish to be involved with the police because you have not asked me to call them and did not argue with me when I offered to shield you. I know that you are ill because you are gaunt and your clothes do not fit. I know that you burn with a personal desire because a man your age rarely craves money or power and that is what drives most. What is left to cause an old man to become involved with gunfire but still want to live so much that he casts his fate into the river?"

I shook my head ruefully and sipped again at the drink, too tired, too beaten, and too old for this.

"So, would you like to tell me what this was about?" he asked.

"If you tell me what you're about first."

He put his drink aside, looked at his hands then up at

me. "I am Colonel Aureliano Buendia, Cuban National Army, Retired."

"Batista?" I asked.

"Castro," he said. "I left the country in '59 when Fidel started bringing in all the *Comunistas*."

"You one of those anti-Castro activists?"

He laughed. "I ran a liquor store in Tampa for twenty-five years. A few years ago after my wife died, I sold it then retired up here seeking some inexpensive quiet."

"Very out-of-the-way quiet," I said, feeling my head grow heavy as the alcohol weighed upon me on top of the morphine.

"Yes," he said. "I had been up this way before hunting with friends. Land is cheap and taxes low. It was the best way I could think of to make my modest savings last."

"And I'm a retired pathologist," I said, reciprocating. "I'd tell you about what happened, but I think I need to rest for a while."

I tried to stand, but my legs balked at the effort and I sat back down on the chair.

"Of course," he said. He rose and took me by the arm, helping me up.

"It's just all hitting me," I said, feeling dizzy.

"Of course." He helped me back to the bedroom.

"Thank you," I said and lay back on the bed. It was good to lie down.

He turned to leave. "If you need anything, I'll be just outside," he said.

Sleep swept over me. I don't think I lasted until he got out the door.

12

THE day had dawned sunny and cold, the temperature
down in the low thirties, the sky a hard deep blue. The
modest bustle of Litchfield on a weekday morning filled
the streets while we idled in the parking lot of the First
Trust Bank. Benny and I were in the front seats while Latoya sat again in the back.

We were all the worse for wear after yesterday. I had
talked Benny into picking up coffee at the Krispy Kreme
down by the Interstate and now sipped at it hungrily.

"So, it's in the bank?" Benny asked.

I nodded. "In a safe-deposit box."

"Well, then," he said, "here's how it's going to go
down. Latoya here is going to be a good girl and wait in
the car, and you and I are going in and getting what's in the
box." Benny looked a mess, his hair greasy and stringy, his
Scientology T-shirt dirty, the odor of a griddle coming off

of him. "Nothing funny in there or Latoya here will never see her kid again."

"Sure," I said, too tired for any complications.

We climbed out of the car. I stood in the parking lot, suddenly in a sweat and shivering.

Benny looked across the car roof at me. "Man, you look like I feel," he said, then laughed. "Not used to playing hardball, huh?"

"You da man, Benny," I said.

"You got that right," he said, hoisting his trousers. "Let's do this thing."

"I'll need something to put it in," I said.

"Right," he said. He popped the trunk, grabbed a knapsack, and tossed it at me.

We went inside. It was just past nine and the bank had only a few folks waiting at the teller windows. Slim Wingate was working the desk this morning. He looked up as we approached.

"Hey, Nelson," he said, rising to shake my hand. His grip was limp, his skin cool and moist. Slim's father had been Litchfield's only undertaker, and though Slim had left the family business and gone into banking, he still retained the grim, gray, sepulchral air of the mausoleum.

"Hey, Slim," I said. "How's things?"

"Pretty good," he said. "Rates on CDs have gone up a quarter point."

"That's nice," I said. "I need to get into my safe-deposit box."

"Sure," he said. He pulled a ledger out of his top drawer. "If you'll just sign in, I'll take you back."

I sat down and wrote my name into the log. Slim looked at me then up at Benny.

"Oh, Slim, this is, um, Benny . . . LeBlanc. He'd like to go back to the vault with me."

Slim's brow furrowed as he looked Benny's raggedy

self up and down. "Well, you know we can't do that, Nelson, unless Mr. LeBlanc's name is on the account . . . which it isn't."

Benny took a step forward.

"Oh, it's all right, Slim," I said. "Benny's just like family."

"I'm sure he is," Slim said firmly, "but even if he was, he still couldn't go back there with you unless his name was on the account. I couldn't let your mother go back with you. God rest her soul."

Benny looked from me to Slim but said nothing. I had known all along that Slim wouldn't bend on this or any other rule. He had been a hall monitor in junior high and had regularly informed on me and any other kid he'd found without a hall pass despite the fact that it often got his ass kicked after school. There are good Germans everywhere and they keep the trains running.

Benny nodded and looked from me to Slim. "That's cool," he said. "That's okay." He punched me on the shoulder somewhat more than affectionately. "Go for it, Big Guy."

Slim wasn't following this. He looked from me to Benny, then walked with me back to the vault. He pulled back the burnished steel bars that closed off the vault, then went inside, opening the key rack that held the bank's copies of the safe-deposit box keys. He searched for and extracted mine. With it in hand, he led me back to the boxes.

I pulled my keys from my pocket and together we extracted the box. It was the largest type that the bank had—a cumbersome load. I hefted it, and Slim led me back to the little rooms alongside the vault room used for opening the boxes in private. Benny watched the whole time from the lobby, craning his neck to try to keep an eye on us.

Slim opened the door to a room for me. "Let me know when you're done," he said.

I shut the door and sat. My hands shook and my shirt hung limply on me, drenched in my own sweat. I lifted the lid to the box.

Stacks of money filled the box—small bills in bundles, grubby and wrinkled. They had an odor to them, dusty and stale and inky. This was the fruit of my misadventures from the year before. Piles of federal paper stolen from men who had gotten it by selling drugs throughout the cities of the Northeast and the South. I grabbed it by the fistfuls and stuffed it into the knapsack until it could hold no more. Even then, there was still quite a bit left in the box. I pushed the remaining cash to one side and at the bottom of the box lay the little leather-bound notebook and the computer disks I'd also stolen that day.

I picked them up. Worn and dog-eared, the notebook contained pages and pages of neat rows and columns of numbers and figures as one might find in a ledger. The first time I had looked through them, I had taken them for sums recorded to document all the money that had been laundered down the Tenn-Tomm Waterway by our late Mafia friends. A wiser man would have turned all this over to the Feds at the time, but something had told me to hold on to them against a rainy day. The floppies comprised a stack of three disks, each labeled with a few cryptic numbers. I'd never bothered to find out what was on them and had held on to them out of the same ill-considered motives.

I put the floppies back into my hip pocket and stuffed the notebook into my pants. It wasn't clear to me whether Benny knew quite what he was looking for. If the money didn't satisfy him, I could produce the notebook and, for what it was worth, still have the floppies in reserve.

Closing the safe-deposit box, I shouldered the knapsack and stood. Whatever adrenalin had been left over from last

night was long gone and I felt grimy and low. As I opened
the door, I saw Slim talking uncomfortably with Benny in
the lobby. Benny had lit up a cigarette and Slim batted
at the smoke that hung in the air while he pointed toward
the door. Benny nodded behind his shades, half turned away.
When he saw me, Slim brightened and moved toward me.

"Get everything taken care of, Nelson?" he asked in a
harried voice.

"Sure thing, Slim," I said.

He took the safe-deposit box from me and put it back.
"You're friend is certainly . . . different," he said diplomat-
ically.

"He's not my friend really," I said.

"Business, then?" Slim asked. He seemed very much
the undertaker inquiring about the dearly departed.

"I guess you could say that."

"Well, I told him we don't allow smoking here, but he
seems to have his own ideas," Slim said primly.

"He's from California," I said. "I think everybody
smokes out there."

Slim rolled his eyes and walked with me out of the
vault. "I've heard they do worse than that," he said. There
was the faintest lilt to this last comment and I suddenly had
pause to wonder about the roots of Slim's bachelorhood.
Perhaps he knew more about what they do out in California than he could own up to here.

"Thanks, Slim," I said, coming out into the lobby.

Benny eyed me evenly, sizing up my knapsack. "Got
it?" he asked.

I nodded. We turned and walked out to the car.

WE sat back in the Mercedes. I held the knapsack in my
lap. Latoya leaned forward from the backseat.

"Let's have it," Benny said.

I tossed it to him sharply. He caught it, undid the top strap, and opened it. Piles of cash welled up in the open mouth of the pack. Benny dug through it, flicking through the bundles, pushing them aside. The money spilled out of the bag, across his lap, and onto the floor as he searched through the bag. Finally he put the knapsack down.

"Yeah, cash. Right," he said. "Where is it?"

"Where's what?" I asked as innocently as I could.

He pulled the pistol out from his belt. "Don't fuck with me. Where is it?"

"Where's what, goddamnit?" I shouted back.

Holding the gun to my head, he said evenly, "Don't fuck with me."

I looked at him. Somewhere behind the sunglasses lay those small dead eyes. An unwashed funk came off of him. I had no idea what he was capable of. I reached under my shirt and pulled the notebook out of my pants.

He grabbed it from me and set the gun down in his lap. "Fuckin-A," he said, flipping through the pages while he stuffed the money back into the knapsack.

"The cash is just pin money compared to this," he said, holding the notebook. "This is the real gold."

"What is it?" I asked.

He looked at me, incredulous. I returned his gaze blankly.

"You really don't know?" he asked. Then he laughed. "But, then, why the hell else would you sit on this and do nothing for the past year?"

"It's a log book," I said, "a balance sheet. Like a ledger."

"Sure," he said. "Good guess."

Through the driver's side window I saw someone turn the corner and approach from the sidewalk—a dark, beefy man in a shiny suit simultaneously too stylish and tacky for these environs. As he walked toward us, from inside his coat he produced a pistol.

"Shit," I said, pointing past Benny toward the approaching form.

"Oh, good one," Benny said. "Like I'm gonna fall for that."

I ducked as the man with the gun fired. The window shattered and a bloom of red exploded from Benny's head. Latoya shrieked. The smell of gun smoke filled the car.

"Fuck!" Benny said, holding the left side of his head, blood streaming between his fingers.

The man fired again, but the round went wide as Benny pushed the knapsack aside, picked up the gun from his lap, and in one move opened his car door and shoulder-rolled onto the street. He came up firing and bellowing.

Latoya shrieked again. Benny fired again, standing beside the car. "Fuck!" he shouted.

From the floorboards of the passenger seat I saw the keys to the Mercedes hanging in the ignition. Footsteps crunched on the gravel of the parking lot as Benny gave chase to whoever had fired on him. Now was my chance.

I climbed off the floor and into the driver's seat.

"What are you doing?" Latoya asked.

"Getting the hell out of here," I said, cranking over the engine.

The car thrummed to life. I dropped it into reverse and popped the clutch. The tires spun as I swerved out of the parking space. Benny turned toward the sound of the car, still holding his ear, blood running between his fingers. He lowered the gun with his other hand.

"Don't do it, Ingram!" he shouted.

I straightened the wheel, pushed it into first, and popped the clutch again. Benny fired wide as we peeled out of the parking lot. The car bottomed out as we bounced onto the street, then I pushed the accelerator to the floor and sped away.

The pop of gunfire came to me distantly. In the rearview mirror, Benny stood braced against the trunk of a parked car, his pistol in a double grip, blood running down his neck. The muzzle flashed and the round slapped into the rear of the car.

"Shit!" Latoya said.

Another shot flashed from his gun as I swerved to the left and skidded around a corner and out of sight.

"Are you crazy?" she shouted.

I eased off on the gas, but continued to screech around corners, putting as much ground as I could between Benny and us.

"Those were guns they were firing back there," I said, "in case you didn't notice."

She climbed over from the backseat as I drove and fell into the passenger seat beside me. "He's got Little Reggie," she said.

"Where?" I asked.

She looked out the back window. "In L.A.," she said. "Somewhere. I don't know."

"After Benny had gotten what he wanted, he was going to kill us both," I said. Only now did I become aware of my heart banging away in my chest as I heaved air in and out. I eased off the gas, my hands shaking.

"What are we gonna do?" she asked.

"I think we should go to the police," I said.

"No," she said, suddenly vehement. "You can't do that."

"Like hell."

"Listen," she said. "Whoever shot Benny knew enough to stake out the bank. They'll probably be waiting near the police station too. We need some time to think about this."

"I don't need any time to think about it," I said.

She pulled at my sleeve. "Just a little time to think about things. Turn here. Right here." Then she pulled hard at the wheel and we screeched through a right-hand turn.

"Jesus! What are you doing?" I tried to wrestle the wheel back from her, but struggling only seemed to be steering us toward a lamppost. I relented and she completed the turn.

As we skidded around the corner, I took control of the wheel again. We were on State Road 57 on our way out of town. In a couple of minutes we were into the countryside, stands of oak and pine and pasture grass running past.

"Listen," I said, "the time for doing this on our own has passed. We need to take this to the police. That man we spoke to last night is with the FBI. He can help us."

"Fuck that," she said. "Like they're gonna break a sweat looking for some nigger widow's kidnapped baby in Compton. Turn here," she said, pointing to a dirt road coming up on the right.

I slowed and rolled down the narrow track. "Just where the hell are we going?" I asked.

"Someplace to lay low and figure out what we're doing," she said.

The knapsack sat on the floor between my knees. The notebook lay on the floorboards beside it. I reached down and picked them both up, put the pack in my lap, and stuffed the notebook inside. The dirt road wound through a thicket of young trees and after about a quarter mile into a clearing, where an old house trailer sat on concrete blocks.

"Who lives here?" I asked.

"Nobody," she said.

We came to a stop in the clearing. I climbed out of the car, shouldered the knapsack, and walked slowly around the clearing. Latoya stood beside the car. The trailer sat crookedly on the cinder blocks, its aluminum siding corroding, its roof sagging under a thick layer of fallen branches and leaves. Decaying garbage, rusting cans, worn shoes, an old hot water heater littered the yard. It was a forlorn place.

"What is this place?" I asked.

She walked up the rickety steps to the trailer and pushed open the door. "One of Reggie's uncles used to live here," she said from the landing and went inside. I followed her up the steps.

She stood in the trailer's front room, looking around sadly. It reeked of mildew, grease, and the funk of years.

"Reggie used to bring me here when we'd had enough of his mama's house. His uncle had died a couple of years before and left this place abandoned." She peered into the bedroom, where a mattress lay on the floor with gray sheets twisted and rumpled across it. "We'd make love in there," she said. "God, it was creepy. But hot, too."

She stood awkwardly. Her eyes were wide, her nostrils flared. She moved toward me. Her scent was strong— musky and sweaty. Those almond eyes looked up at me. I pulled at the air, suddenly breathless. She drew me down to her, her lips on mine. God, I tasted her and pulled her close.

My heart pounded in my chest. All of the last two days, the deaths, the gunshots, and shabbiness of our surrounding, faded from memory and I knew only her. For the past year she'd haunted my dreams and now she was in my arms. I sighed and buried my face in the nape of her neck, inhaling her, holding her to me.

"Well, isn't this cute?" came a voice from behind me.

We broke apart and I turned. Benny stood in the open door of the trailer, bare-chested, holding a pistol in one hand and his T-shirt pressed to his bleeding ear with the other hand.

Latoya stood back from me.

"Bleeding's almost stopped," he said, sliding down against one wall of the trailer, dabbing at the side of his head. "Car-jacked a pickup from some poor cracker."

I looked from him to Latoya and back.

Seeing my confusion, he laughed. "Sorry to disappoint you, Nelson, but she's with me. This is where we were supposed to meet up if the shit hit the fan and we got separated."

"All that stuff about Little Reggie?"

She looked away. Benny laughed again. "She said you were a sucker for a sob story. Man, we played you like a fiddle. If our mob friend hadn't fucked things up for us at the bank, we'd still be playing you."

Latoya walked into the next room. Benny stood and moved to the bathroom, uncovering his bloody ear and inspecting it in the mirror. The gun lay across the edge of the sink.

"This town's about to get a little too hot for us," he said. "I left that greaseball gut-shot on the street. We're gonna have to make tracks. But I'm gonna need some medical supplies to take care of this."

He turned and tossed the truck keys to Latoya. "There's a pharmacy I saw about two miles down the road at the edge of town. You need to get some four-by-fours and gauze and silk tape . . . and some peroxide. I'll stay and watch Jimmie Olson here."

"I need something first," she said sadly.

He looked at her, then pulled a small metal vial from his pocket. Making a fist, he tapped some white powder into the hollow at the base of his thumb. She bent over and snorted it up quickly, then licked the residue up.

"Is that how you got her?" I asked Benny. "Coke?"

He looked at me. The gun still lay on the edge of the sink behind him. "Just one of the perks," he said.

"Hey, 'Toya," he went on, "bring me my suitcase from

the trunk of the Benz before you leave. I need a change of clothes."

Latoya headed out the door to the car, not able to meet my eyes.

Seeing my amazement and confusion, Benny couldn't keep from laughing aloud, still holding his bloody shirt to his head.

"Ingram, you have no idea what you've gotten yourself into."

13

LACY sat across from me at the table. She was gaunt and bald and her eyes were dull and faraway. She reached out a bony arm toward me.

"Seymour," she said, "this shouldn't be so hard."

"I know," I said. "I don't know what to say."

She smiled, her face becoming a ragged document of fissures and valleys, her blue eyes brightening briefly. "There's nothing you can say. Just stop holding it against God."

"Who else do I have to hold it against?" I asked.

She shook her head.

"I don't know what to do," I said.

"Don't be afraid," she said, "you'll be here soon."

I could smell her perfume. Chanel No. 5. It was so good to see her and speak with her even as ill as she looked. I knew it was a dream even while dreaming it, but I fought waking up, wanting it to last.

When I woke, it was late into the morning, the sun already high in the sky and shining through the windows of the bedroom. The smell of coffee hung in the air. Lying still beneath these clean sheets, my back didn't hurt, but my heart ached at the memory of Lacy. I had been like an unmoored ship since she'd passed. I'd never have gotten into this mess had she been around to keep me sane.

I rolled to my side and the pain in my back came roaring back. On the bedside table I saw my pill bottle standing beside a glass of water—my immediate-release morphine, the container looking worse for wear after its trip with me down the river. I took two tablets, washing them down with the water, lying back again on the bed waiting for them to take hold.

Hate and narcotics were all I had left. It would all be over soon one way or the other. They would have to be enough for now.

From the far room I could make out voices going to and fro in a steady rhythm. Outside, a breezed rustled through the trees and a chorus of birds chirped and rattled. Goddamn Mother Nature carrying on again as if things were just fine. The problem with nature was it had no sense of history, no sense of the tragic. The earth cracks open, volcanoes erupt, the forests burn, and the next day out of the ash and rubble some damn daisy sprouts, cheerfully oblivious to all that has come before, ready to give it another try.

After perhaps half an hour I rolled out of bed and stood, the pain awful but bearable. I pulled the bathrobe around me and surveyed the room. The door seemed a challenging distance away, but I took one step and then another, teetering.

The door swung open as I leaned into it and I was out into the cabin's main room. He looked up from where he sat at his kitchen table and smiled.

"Awake at last," he said.

I nodded and hobbled over to the table, sitting gratefully beside him on one of the old vinyl upholstered steel-tube chairs. "What time is it?" I asked.

"Almost noon," he said.

"That coffee?" I asked, staring at the mug he held in his hands.

"Excuse me," he said, rising and pouring me a cup from the coffeepot on the kitchen counter.

"Cream or sugar?" he asked, setting it in front of me.

"Black," I said.

He sat back down at his place. "So, you were going to tell me how it was that you washed up on my bank last night."

I looked at him. His was a pleasant face, dark and open, gray hair framing his bald head. Brown eyes watched me intently, missing nothing. He looked like much more than a retired liquor store owner. I sipped at the coffee—it was rich and dark, but subtle. Sort of like him. I had nothing to lose, so I laid it all out for him—Nelson's hijinks of last year, my prostate cancer, William's murder, the hit man from last night, the fire. He listened closely. I must have gone on for thirty minutes and he only added an occasional nod and word of sympathy. When I had finished, he sat back in his chair.

"Normally I would find this all very hard to believe," he said.

I shrugged. "Suit yourself."

"In your case, though, I'm moved to accept what you say at face value."

I shrugged again. "Suit yourself either way."

He smiled. "So, you are on a quest for revenge like Captain Ahab?"

I returned his gaze evenly. "You could say so."

"Can I do anything to help you?" he asked.

"Get me back to my house so I can get my car and some of my things."

He nodded. "And what do I tell the police if they come calling?"

"Tell them what you please, just get me out of here first."

He stood. "Let me get you your clothes. I washed them out last night. They should be dry by now."

The pants and shirt were still damp but I pulled them on. We went out to his car—a Chevy pickup a few years old. The day was clear and cool, the sun shining but distant. Through the trees I could see Nelson's lot. A sheriff's car sat there and a couple of officers stood beside it.

He drove glancing over at me regularly. I sat leaning against the car door, giving him directions from time to time, wondering what I was going to do next.

"So I laid myself bare," I said at last to fill out the silence "Why don't you tell me about yourself?"

He glanced over at me again, smiling. "There's not much to say."

"I find that hard to believe."

He stared ahead at the road. "I was with Fidel in the early days. Soon after they came ashore on the *Granma* and went into the mountains."

"Really?"

"It was a different time," he said. "I was very young. Fidel was like a Christ to us. We would have done anything for him. I could tell you many stories."

He drove for a few moments in silence. "But after Batista fled and we came into Havana, things changed very rapidly. Democracy was what we fought for, but before we knew it . . . we became what we had beheld. I left the country by boat."

"I'd like to hear more about that," I said.

"Someday perhaps," he said. "I spent the next twenty-five years in Tampa."

"Sort of an anticlimax?"

He sighed. "America is a great country. But my heart will always be with Cuba. Someday perhaps Fidel will be gone and I can go back."

"These backwoods seem like a funny place to find a man like you," I said.

He nodded. "And you?" he asked. "What are you really going to do?"

"I don't know yet," I said. "I need to find out what went up in that fire last night. I have a feeling that whoever killed William didn't."

After another twenty minutes of driving, we came up to my house. The Suburban still sat outside the garage where I'd left it. We rolled up to the front door. He shut off the engine and we both climbed out. A yellow CRIME SCENE tape was strung across the front door. I ripped it down, unlocked the door, and we both went inside.

The front room held the detritus of the criminals' and police's work from the day before—pulled-out drawers, paper wrappers, gray splotches where they'd dusted for fingerprints. I stood just inside the doorway. The house seemed dead, the air stagnant and stale, the smell of William's blood still coming to me.

"Very nice," the colonel said, looking around.

"Yeah," I grumbled, walking toward my bedroom. "I need a change of clothes." I turned back to him. "Thank you for your help, but I can take it from here."

He nodded, smiling. "You're welcome," he said, but just stood there.

"Thank you," I said. "I'll be fine."

"I know," he said. "If I could just make a telephone call?"

"Sure," I said, pointing to the phone amid the rubble in the living room.

In the bedroom the same litter lay scattered across the floor. I pulled on some clean clothes. My shirt and pants gapped loosely around me.

I sat on the bed, feeling old and sore and tired. Christ, what was I going to do? What could I do?

Not having the nerve to go into the bathroom, I went into the kitchen to wash up.

The colonel still stood in the living room, standing beside the phone. He turned as I came in.

"I think I can be of some help to you," he said.

I walked past him into the kitchen. "How's that?" I asked, bending over the sink.

"Someone within the Mafia seems to be after you. I have friends in Tampa who may be able to find out who is behind it."

"Some friends," I said, washing my hands and face.

He stood in the doorway to the kitchen. "Perhaps I did a little more than sell liquor. I have some contacts from those days."

I looked at him as I toweled off. "Why don't you just come clean and tell what you're really all about?"

He smiled awkwardly and looked at his shoes. "I have worked against Fidel during my time here in America. From that I have gotten to know many different people from different lines of work. In my retirement, I wanted a place that was very much out of the way so that all of these people could not easily visit me."

"I see." God knows what this fellow had been into, but perhaps he could be of some use. "Why don't you make your calls and see what you can find out."

"I made my first call while you were changing. Trafficante's people in Tampa may be behind this."

"Trafficante?"

"He was the head of organized crime in Florida. His people were the ones backing the money-laundering operation that you and Mr. Ingram stumbled into last year. They are the ones most interested in exacting revenge on you both."

"What else can you find out? Can you tell me who specifically these people are and where I can find them? I don't want some middleman or lieutenant. I want the man at the top."

"I will make additional calls and learn what I can," he said.

"I need to make a call first," I said. I picked up the phone in the kitchen and called the Litchfield Police Department.

"Officer Trottman, please," I said to the woman who answered the phone.

"Who may I say is calling?" she asked.

"Dr. Seymour Hartley," I said.

"One moment," she said and put me on hold.

Sonny picked up a second later. "Seymour!" he said. "Goddamn, where are you? We thought you were dead."

"I did, too," I said. "I need to know if any bodies were found in Ingram's cabin after it burned."

"No," he said, "No bodies. Now tell me where you are."

"Do you have any leads?"

"No," he said. "That FBI agent Edmonds is all over our asses but he don't know nothin'."

"Just tell everyone I'm okay and to leave me alone."

"Now, goddamnit, Seymour, you're a material witness to two or three crimes. You can't just take off."

"That's not how I read the Constitution," I said.

"Listen, Seymour," he went on, "there was a shooting this morning outside the First Trust Bank. There's some dangerous shit coming down around you."

"What do you mean 'a shooting'?"

"Guns, Seymour. Bullets. There's some Yankee lying dead on the sidewalk right after your friend Ingram withdrew something from his safe-deposit box."

"Where's Nelson now?"

"No one knows. Last seen with that colored girl heading out of town in a Mercedes."

"Thanks, Sonny," I said. "I'll keep my head down."

"Damnit," he said, "just tell me where you are and I'll send an officer out."

"I'll be in touch." And I hung up.

"Make your calls," I said to the colonel, "then we have to get out of here unless we want to deal with the police and the FBI." I handed him the phone. "I'll be in the garage getting some things."

He took the receiver from me.

"Just why are you doing this?" I asked him. "It could be very dangerous."

He looked at his feet again. "Retirement is less than I had hoped for," he said. "I am a widower and my children are estranged from me. I need something to keep me alive."

"Sounds familiar," I said. I left him with the phone in the kitchen and went to the garage.

My Lincoln sat there in the garage. I hadn't driven it in months. I wondered if William had been turning it over once in a while to keep the battery from going flat. I opened its door and sat down. The leather of the seats, the floor mats and carpets, the dash were all spotless. I pulled out my keys and cranked it over. It started right up.

Tears stung the back of my eyes. William had taken such good care of me and I had gone and gotten him killed. While he had been around, I'd been a self-absorbed shit, dwelling on the loss of Lacy and my prostate cancer. I had barely noticed him and had certainly given him little credit for his grief over the loss of his own wife. And I felt doubly guilty because of how much better I felt now with his revenge as my business.

I shut the car off and went back to the gun cabinet. Unlocking it, I pulled out another 9mm. I stood back and looked at the collection of weapons, vaguely embarrassed by the assemblage. What was a grown man doing with so many obviously useless and dangerous toys? Except that they'd been far from useless in the past year. God knows what had motivated me to acquire all this. Boredom, paranoia, insanity. And now here I was getting them out again. How had it come to this, and why did it make me feel good when nothing else in life did?

I walked back to the kitchen, where the colonel waited.

"Find out anything?" I asked.

"A little," he said. "They are after something more than revenge."

I nodded. "The man I interrogated last night at Ingram's cabin mentioned something about finding out what we knew. He said he was sent by Frank Losurdo."

"Trafficante's man," the colonel said. "And where is Ingram now?"

"I don't know. He's kind of missing. There was a shooting downtown right after he withdrew something from a safe-deposit box."

"I'd say the trail to those you seek goes through Ingram. And we've got to get to him before these people or the police do."

"But how're we going to do that?"

He was all business. "We'll need some things."

14

W ITHIN an hour we were on the road again in the stolen pickup truck, heading out of the county on back roads. After Latoya had returned from the drugstore, she and Benny had cleaned and dressed his ear, concealing the dressing under a knit watch cap. Now the three of us sat side by side in the truck with my right wrist tied to the metal frame of the seat.

"We got to ditch this thing and get us a ride that isn't quite so hot," Benny said as he drove. "Police are gonna be all over this license plate."

"Next time boost something that's got a little more style," Latoya said. "This piece of shit's too redneck for me."

"Where are we going?" I asked.

"You'd better hope it's somewhere a long way off, 'cause your usefulness to me will be pretty much over when we get there," Benny said.

We were headed south, which would take us deeper and

deeper into nowhere—a hundred miles of two-lane roads and farmland.

"So where *are* we going?" Latoya asked.

"Fuck!" Benny said, steering with one hand and leaning over the both of us to rummage through the glove box. "There's gotta be some road maps in here. How do you get back to the Interstate from here?"

The pickup drifted down onto the shoulder of the road.

"Shit," Latoya said, pushing the wheel and steering back onto the road.

"Maybe Andy of Mayberry here will tell us how to get out of here," Benny said.

"Just turn around," I said. "This road will take you straight back to Litchfield."

"Christ," he went on, "if I see another cow, I'm gonna scream. Where's the nearest town?"

"You just passed it," I said. "That brick bungalow back there was Turner's Corners."

Benny shook his head. "Fuck me," he said.

On we drove through increasingly desolate fields and fen. Clouds blew in from the south as the afternoon lengthened. My head pounded, I was grimy and unwashed and in no mood for this. The miles rolled past, somehow managing to grow ever emptier and more godforsaken—shotgun shacks, rusted-out cars, and fallow tracts. Here and there children stood in yards and along the road, boggling at our passage as if they were watching apparitions.

"Where does this goddamn road go?" Benny asked.

"Pretty much nowhere," I said. "The only good thing to say about it is that it'll take the sheriff a long time to get officers out here. You're not likely to run into many road blocks."

"Great," he said. "We're hiding out in the asshole of the universe."

"We're headed south," I said. "There's nothing much between us and Mobile."

"I need to get to a phone," he said.

"And I got to pee," Latoya said.

After another half-hour of driving, a cluster of buildings on either side of the road declared the encounter with another little town—a closed gas station flanked by a cinderblock bar with a red neon Budweiser sign beckoning from its window.

"This'll do," Benny said, pulling into the bar's parking lot. He turned off the truck, then handed his gun to Latoya. "You watch him. I'll be right back."

"No way," Latoya said. "I got to pee."

"Give me a minute, goddamnit," he said. "I've got to make this call."

Benny climbed out and Latoya scooted over behind the steering wheel, facing me with her back against the door, the pistol cradled between her legs.

"Don't look at me like that," she said.

"I just don't understand," I said.

She snorted. "You think you did me a favor saving my ass and giving me all that money? Shit. I'd'a been better off dead."

"What? You'd have rather been murdered by the mob?"

"Maybe," she said. "Maybe it'd be better than putting up with all this shit."

"So where is Little Reggie really?"

She looked down at her hands. "You think I don't care?" Looking up, her eyes burning, she said, "You think I just pissed him away? He's why I'm doing this. Benny says this'll be a really big score. Not like that chump change you laid on me last year."

"What happened?"

"Reggie's safe," she went on. "He's with my momma in L.A."

"But where'd all the money go?"

"It went, man," she said. "It fucking went." She shook her head. "Car. Clothes. Trips. Blow."

"Where'd you meet this Benny creep?"

"Like I said. At college. I did try. I really did try to make good."

"Then he showed up?"

"He knew all these people. We went to parties. Courtside at the Lakers. For the first time since Reggie and me left L.A., I was having fun. Then the next thing I know, the money's all gone and I got debts to people you don't want to owe money to, and Benny has cooked up this plan." She started crying.

"What's the plan?"

She smiled in a grimacing way. "I don't really know. There's supposed to be this big score at the end of it all. Something about mob money and bank accounts. I don't know. He had heard about all your bullshit last year. I told him you were a sucker for a hard luck story, so we came down here to see if we could play you for what you knew."

Benny came out of the bar and walked back to the truck. He pulled open the driver's door. "He behaving himself?" he asked.

"Trying to bullshit me," she said.

"He can bullshit me for a while now. You go in and pee."

She climbed out and Benny climbed in, taking the pistol from her.

"So what if I got to pee?" I asked.

"We'll stop in the woods later," he said. He reached down into the knapsack where it sat on the floorboards and pulled out the notebook.

"So what's in there?" I asked.

He looked at me. "I can't believe you sat on this for a year and had no idea what you had."

"How did you know that I had it or what it was?"

"I knew people who knew people. This bust last year was some heavy shit. Set off ripples, pissed people off, got people talking."

"What kind of people?"

He snorted. "The wrong kind of people. The kind of people who were sending that money down to Central America in the first place."

"So what's in the book?"

He slapped it against his thigh. "The son-of-a-bitch who was running the operation for the mob was skimming off the top. All the millions and millions he sent downstream to be laundered, he skimmed a few percent for himself and cooked the books. Got so pissed off when you started sniffing around that he came down here to head off trouble and got himself killed in the process. This is his ledger. And in the back are account numbers. Swiss bank account numbers."

"How much is there?"

"Don't know. But it's gotta be a lot. Millions." He turned to the back of the notebook. "Now all I gotta do is find the account numbers."

"How do you know there are account numbers?" I asked, craning to look at the book over his shoulder.

"I was told there were Swiss accounts," he said.

"Really?"

He looked at me, clearly annoyed. "Yeah, asshole. Really." He pondered the back pages of the notebook. "Somewhere in here."

"Looks like just a bunch of numbers to me."

He flipped back and forth between the pages.

Latoya walked up to the truck and stood beside the driver's window.

"Yo," she said, "We got visitors."

Benny looked up from the notebook. "Where?"

"Behind you."

He looked up in the rearview mirror. "Fucking great," he said.

I looked out the back window of the pickup. A sheriff's cruiser rolled into the parking lot behind us.

"I thought you said that the sheriff'd be a long time getting out this far," Benny said.

"Well, you drove off into Colequit County," I said. "So I guess maybe I was wrong."

"Funny guy," he said. "Act up now and you're dead."

The cruiser pulled up beside us, and a deputy climbed out.

"What are we gonna do?" Latoya asked, looking innocently out at the roadway.

Benny tucked his pistol under his thigh and smiled and looked back at Latoya. "Just follow my lead."

The deputy walked around the back of the truck with his pistol drawn.

"Morning," he said, leaning against the side of the truck bed, bracing his gun arm on it. "I wonder if y'all could step away from the truck and keep your hands in the air."

Latoya stood back, held her hands up, her eyes big as saucers.

"Why, certainly, Officer," Benny said, climbing out of the truck, holding one hand up but the other holding his gun behind his thigh.

"Both hands," the deputy said nervously to Benny.

"Sure thing," Benny said, smiling broadly. He brought the gun up and fired.

The deputy sagged to his left, hit. In the next instant, Benny took a big step forward, blocked the deputy's pistol off to the side with his left arm, and brought him down with a kick to the leg. He tucked his gun into his pants, reached down, and tossed the deputy's gun to Latoya.

"If you're gonna pack deadly force, you gotta be ready to use it," he said to the deputy.

He hauled him back to his feet. The deputy grimaced.

"Now," Benny said, "I'm trying very hard not to kill anyone else today. If you come with me quietly, I will continue to try not to kill you."

Benny nodded at Latoya and they all walked together back to the bar, the deputy hobbling on Benny's arm, leaving me alone tied to the seat of the pickup. Nothing stirred outside in the wake of the shooting. After a few minutes, the neon BUD sign in the window switched off and the OPEN sign was flipped over to a red CLOSED sign. Benny and Latoya walked back out of the door.

Benny climbed into the patrol car, poked around inside, then popped the trunk and checked it out. Latoya pulled their luggage out of the back of the truck and carried them over to the car's trunk. Just as I was starting to hope they'd leave me behind, they came over and opened the truck's passenger door.

"Left him and the owner of the bar handcuffed to the toilet," Benny said as he covered me with the gun and Latoya untied me. "It should take them a while to get loose."

"If he don't bleed to death first," she added.

"Nah," Benny said. "I just got him through the muscle. Soon as he bleeds down a little, his pressure will drop low enough so it'll clot off. Seen it a dozen times."

We walked over to the patrol car. The roadway was deserted. No one had apparently witnessed our little scene. Latoya sat behind the wheel with Benny beside her holding a gun on me as I climbed into the back.

Benny smiled. "Officer Opie has been so kind as to provide us with the perfect set of wheels to get us out of this goddamn place. Now we can go back the way we came straight through Litchfield to the Interstate and get the hell out of here."

15

A TRIP to the Radio Shack at the mall landed us a police radio scanner, then a visit to the hunting and tackle store turned up USGS maps of the county. The colonel and I sat in his truck in the parking lot of the store, listening to the radio crackle while we studied the maps unfolded between us, peering at the county's roads and highways.

"The bank where the shooting took place is here," I said, pointing toward its approximate location in downtown Litchfield.

"He was running," he said. "He would want to get out of town quickly."

"Then he would have gone out on Highway 57," I said, tapping the map. "It runs straight out into the county, then on to Colequit County. It's a good place to get lost."

He pondered the map. "Is he running from something or toward something?"

"Away. There are some pretty bad people on his trail."

"Then he will try to hide. Is there anyplace out there that he knows?"

I thought for a few moments. "Acres and acres of trailers and rusted-out cars and used-up cotton fields. Poor blacks and white trash. That Mercedes-Benz'll stick out like a sore thumb."

It was then that we heard the bulletin on the scanner about a pickup truck car-jacked and stolen just after the shooting at the bank.

"Perhaps they are not driving a Mercedes now," the colonel said.

"If we're going to get to them before the police, we're going to have to be a step ahead of everyone," I said.

He nodded, folded the maps over, and started the truck.

The afternoon had turned cool, the sun in a hazy blue sky. We drove out of town, passing by the First Trust Bank on the way. Police lines were all around it with a couple of patrol cars parked in front. I thought I could pick out that fellow from the FBI standing there, looking about disgustedly, hands on his hips.

In a few minutes, we were out into the county. The colonel drove at a leisurely pace and we both looked out into the woods and fields.

"Really, why are you doing this?" I asked him.

He glanced at me, then shrugged. "I told you," he said. "I have little else to do with myself."

"Out of such feelings one might take up bird watching or taxidermy, but not usually vigilante justice."

He smiled but said nothing. "I need a cause," he said at last.

"I thought you were fighting Fidel."

"Once. But it came to nothing. The old man seems immortal now. Stalin, Mao, Ho, Kruschev, Brezhnev are all gone. Communism itself will soon be gone, but Fidel just goes on. Cuba is like a sleeper caught in Fidel's nightmare.

Someday they will awaken to find that the Old Man has devoured the fields, drunk up the ocean, and breathed in all the air and consumed time itself. I am afraid that when I am able to go back, nothing will be left."

"That's communism," I said. "When it can't remake reality in its own image, it settles instead for emptying the world of everything else. Genocide is the end of all utopian dreams."

He looked at me. "A philosopher, I see."

"Had my flirtation with Marx and Lenin."

He shook his head sadly as he drove. "So, instead, we stay here in America and dream of Marilyn and Jack and James Dean."

"And Elvis. They're better dreams."

16

L ATOYA drove us back toward Litchfield. Benny sat smoking in the front seat. He began flipping again through the notebook.

"I looked at that book before I put it away," I said to him. "I never saw any account numbers."

He raised his shades and looked at me hard. He couldn't find them either.

"Lots of figures all added up, but I didn't see anything more than that," I said.

"In the back," he said, sounding unconvinced. He held up the notebook, showing a page of number and letter combinations.

"Could be phone numbers for all I can see," I said.

"It's in code," he said. "It's gotta be."

"You know there was something else that I took along with the money and that notebook," I said.

He stared at me hard again. "Bullshit," he said.

I looked out the window. "Okay, it's bullshit." I could feel him still watching me.

"What else?" he asked.

"Nothing," I said. "It's bullshit."

"Don't fuck with me," he said, bringing the gun over the seat and waving it in my direction.

I grabbed the gun and wrenched Benny's hand down over the back of the seat, leaning hard on it. He held his grip and began to wrestle with me. I brought my free hand around and hit him backhand on his ear.

"Shit!" Benny said, falling back and letting go of the gun.

Latoya hit the brakes. Benny piled into the dash and I fell forward. The car screeched and veered into a four-wheel drift headed for the shoulder.

"Fuck!" she said.

The car slid sideways into the trees off the shoulder, a branch crashing through the driver's-side rear window. Glass shattered as Benny bellowed and the car skidded to a stop. In the next second, the racket and screaming were replaced by a stunned silence. The car was full of dust and falling leaves. I sat wedged between the front and back seats on the floorboards. Latoya struggled with the gun Benny had given her. I reached over and took it from her, then picked up Benny's gun from the floorboards.

Pushing myself up onto the backseat, I brought both pistols to bear. "Now, both you assholes get out of the car."

"Fuck," Benny said. He cracked open the passenger door and rolled onto the dirt, holding the side of his head. Latoya climbed out after him, clambering over him to stand on the shoulder. I pushed open the rear door and stood.

"Both of you get over there and lie facedown on the dirt, arms out wide," I said. "Now."

Benny looked up at me. "You've got me pissed now, you son-of-a-bitch."

I fired a round into the ground at his feet. "Well, you've been pissing me off for days, so don't push your luck."

He stood up. "I'm gonna kill you." From under his watch cap, blood ran from his ear and down his neck.

"In case you haven't noticed, I'm the one with the gun right now." I took a step back and put the trunk of the patrol car between us.

He paused, considering the odds.

"You're not the only one here who's killed a man," I said.

He turned his head and spat, then took a few steps toward the shoulder of the road. Grabbing Latoya, he pushed her at me, ducked down, and dashed into the woods. I raised the gun, tracked him for a second, then he was gone among the trees.

I pulled the knapsack out of the car. The notebook lay loose on the floorboards in the front. I grabbed it and stuffed it in the pack. I sat on the hood of the car and took a deep breath, feeling better than I had in days. Latoya stood there looking at me.

"We need to get out of here," I said.

"What are you going to do with me?" she asked.

"I don't know," I said. "Get back behind the wheel."

I tucked one of the guns into my belt. Latoya climbed in the passenger's side and crawled behind the wheel. I scanned the woods then climbed in after her.

"Let's go," I said.

She glowered at me then cranked the starter. Putting it in reverse, she backed out, the branches scraping the side and snapping where they poked through the broken window. In a moment we were back on the road.

"Where we going?" she asked.

"South," I said, "to State Road 19." I sat against the passenger door, the gun in my lap, watching her.

"What are you going to do with me?" she asked again.

"I don't know yet," I said. "I need time to figure things out."

"So, then, where are we going? To the police?"

"Not yet. Just drive."

17

WE drove down Highway 57. It had turned into another goddamn beautiful fall afternoon. My back hurt like a bitch despite having enough morphine onboard to kill a horse. The colonel drove his pickup at a gradual pace and we scanned the road while the radio played country-western.

"Patsy Cline," he said, turning up the volume. "The Queen."

Shit. I'd spent my whole life down here and was as Southern as country ham, but I still couldn't abide country music. It affirmed every cliché and backward notion that's kept the South in poverty and ignorance for a hundred and twenty years.

"Yeah," I said. "The Queen." We drove on. On either side were empty fields and corroded trailers, silent confirmation of the country ballad's laments.

Halfway to the horizon down this ruler-straight road a figure could be seen standing on the shoulder. The colonel picked him out too. We both watched his approach. As he came into the middle distance, we could see he was hitch-hiking.

The colonel took his foot off the gas and slowed. I peered ahead. There was something familiar about him.

"I know him," I said. It was that little peckerwood who rode into Nelson's fish camp the day before. What the hell was his name? Barry? Lenny? Some goddamn California name.

"He's hitchhiking," the colonel said.

"Let's pick him up," I said. "I saw him yesterday at Nelson's house. Let's play our cards close and see what he knows."

The colonel braked and steered for the shoulder. The peckerwood brightened and ran after us as we passed him and came to a stop.

He dashed up to the driver's side of the truck. Instead of the Scientololgy T-shirt from yesterday, he wore one that read HONK IF YOU LOVE JESUS. He had a watch cap pulled down over his head, sunglasses over his eyes, and a dried trickle of blood down the side of his neck.

"Gawd-dahmn," he said, "am Ah glad thet yew two fellers came along!" He sounded as if he's learned his Southern at the Foghorn Leghorn School of Diction, eliding his *r*'s and dropping the *g*'s at the ends of his partici-ples like a cross-breed between a Kentucky colonel and Oklahoma trailer trash. It was sad that this was how most of the country thought we talked down here.

The colonel nodded. "Hop in," he said.

Barry or Biff or whatever-the-hell his name was charged cheerfully around to the passenger side. I opened the door and climbed out, offering him the middle of the bench seat.

"Much obliged," he said, continuing the down-home ruse.

"Where're you headed?" I asked, trying to match him drawl-for-drawl.

He shook his head. "You wouldn't believe me if I told you. Anywheres toward a town with more'n one horse will do."

"What happened to you there?" I asked, pointing to the blood on his neck.

"Wouldn't believe that either," he said. "Some varmint and his colored girlfriend shot me in the ear and robbed me of every dime I had."

"Do tell?" I asked.

"If I'm lying, I'm dying," he said.

Christ, this was getting hard to listen to.

"So, do you want us to take you to the police?" I asked.

"Thanks," he said, "but I'd rather settle this on my own."

The colonel offered his right hand while steering with his left. "I'm Al Buendia," he said. He nodded in my direction. "And this is Doc."

The peckerwood took his hand and gave it a big pump. "Billy Bob Thornberry," he said, "American by birth and Southern by the Grace of God."

The colonel looked him up and down, smiling, then turned back to his driving.

"So, Al," Billy Bob went on, "noticing that you yourself are a man of color, I hope that you didn't take offense at my remark about the colored girl."

"Don't give a second thought," the colonel said. "The Buendias have always been dark but we are Castilian."

"Sure. You know, there's people of color and then there's colored people, if you catch my drift." He laughed and slapped his knees.

"So where'd these folks who robbed you go?" I asked.

"I wish I knew, Doc," he said. "If I find them, they're sure gonna remember it."

"Well, listen," I said, "if you're trying to get back to town, you're hitchhiking in the wrong direction. This road just takes you pretty much through nowhere until you get to Mobile."

"I need to get to a phone and rent me a car," he said.

I looked over to the colonel. "Hey, Al," I drawled, "what do you say we run this good-ol'boy into Litchfield so he can get some help?"

The colonel smiled. "Why, sure thing," he drawled back as best he could.

"All right!" Billy Bob said. "You two dudes are awesome."

Dudes. Shit.

The colonel swung the truck into a wide U-turn, bumping over both shoulders of the road in the process, and in a moment we were headed back the way we came.

Just then, the police scanner crackled to life again, reported a deputy sheriff down, shot in the leg and handcuffed to the toilet in Demar's Bar and Grill out in Colequit County. And damn if it didn't sound like Nelson's voice.

"That's the guy," Billy Bob said, pointing at the scanner. "He shot the deputy and left him for dead then ran off in his cop car."

"Then why is he calling it in now?" I asked.

"Probably got nervous about killing a cop," Billy Bob said. "Maybe to divert attention while he makes his getaway."

"Demar's Bar and Grill is just down the road back the way we were headed. You want to turn around again and check it out? Maybe tell the police what you know?"

Billy Bob held up his hands. "Thanks, fellas, but the way we're headed is just fine. I got my own issues with the law and I can't get started on them just right now, if you know what I mean."

"Ten-four, good buddy," I said.

"Roger that," the colonel added. We were all so down-home that it seemed perfect when Tammy Wynette came on singing "Stand By Your Man."

"She's the Queen," the colonel said.

"I thought Patsy Cline was the Queen?" I asked.

"And so is Loretta Lynn. They are all Queens."

Two Potter County Sheriff's cars, their blue lights spinning, sped past us headed in the other direction.

"So, is there a place to rent cars in Litchfield?" Billy Bob asked, watching the patrol cars speed away over his shoulder.

I thought for a moment. "There's Teddy Johnson's Exxon down by the Interstate. He rents U-Hauls."

"You mean, like, trucks?"

"Guess so."

"Man. Listen," he said, "there's a road coming up ahead. Do you think you could turn in and drop me off there instead?"

"Where?" the colonel asked.

"Jeez, I dunno," he said, leaning forward and peering out the windshield. "Up ahead. There. Past that little cluster of trees. A left turn."

We braked and rolled down a dirt road. Trees overhung the road. Down the road a few hundred yards we came into a clearing where a Mercedes sat in front of an old trailer. It looked to be the same car that Billy Bob had driven the night before.

"What's this?" I asked.

He'd reached over me, opened the door, and climbed out before the truck had stopped.

"Thanks for the lift," he said. He began to walk toward the car.

I grabbed a pistol from underneath the seat and climbed out after him. Things had gone far enough.

"What is this place?" I asked, coming up behind him.

He turned and saw the gun. "Whoa, Grandad," he said. "I'm just gonna get in my car and go on my way."

"Listen, Billy Bob," I said, "that redneck who you say shot you and stole your car is a friend of mine and he's worth ten of you. Now, I want to know who you are and what you know and what this place is."

He looked around, judging the opportunities. The colonel climbed out of the truck, reached into the back, and pulled out another pistol. Billy Bob watched this and I could see his spirits sag.

"Man," he said, dropping the Southern drawl, "you are some stone crazy people down here."

"My grandfather was black," the colonel said evenly, walking forward, "and I do take what you said personally. If you don't start talking, the good doctor here will let me express how I feel in a more physical idiom." He played the Bad Cop well.

Billy Bob leaned against the back fender of the Mercedes, looking from one of us to the other. "I don't where Ingram is right now," he said. "He took my gun, took the money, and ran off in a sheriff's car."

"What money?"

"Money he stole from the mob last year. That's why they're down here now. One of the son-of-a-bitches shot me in the ear this morning." He smiled. "I fixed his ass."

"And why are you down here?" I asked.

"The money, man."

"How did you find out about it?"

"I got my sources. Latoya was one of them."

"The black girl?" I asked.

"Yeah. She was in on this with him last year."

"Is there anything more than money in this?"

"Like what?" he asked, looking evasive.

"Something else. Seems like there's more than just money behind all this attention."

"Just the money was what brought me here," he said.

"The money was what Nelson took out of the bank this morning?"

He nodded.

"How much was there?"

"A lot. A knapsack full."

"And you don't know where they went?"

He shook his head. "No, man. Now, why don't you just let me get in my car and get out of this damn county. I got my ear shot off, he took my girl and the money, my damn Mercedes is all shot up and bloody. I just want to get out of here."

"Make sure you get," I said. "If I see your face around here again, I won't be so kind."

"Color me gone," he said and climbed into the Mercedes. In a minute he had pulled past us and peeled down the road in a spray of dirt. We both stood looking after him.

"Where do we go from here?" the colonel finally asked.

"Still gotta find that varmint Ingram," I said, turning back toward the truck.

18

AFTER I called in the report of the wounded officer, I figured I had about a half an hour until they started looking for a stolen Colequit County Sheriff's car. We crept back into Potter County by the hindmost of back roads, in a couple of cases down dirt roads that were little better than cow paths.

My intimate knowledge of these environs, I hoped, was one of my greatest assets in our current predicament. After Benny had run off, I'd considered going straight to the police, but the memory of last year when the law had proven a false friend and the thought of this morning when I was shot at outside my own bank gave me pause about going back into Litchfield. I had thought of lighting out for the territories and trying to disappear into some other lost corner of the county. But then I would be truly alone looking for enemies behind every bush and bereft of allies or friends. I needed time to consider my options and to figure out what I had that people seemed so intent upon. What better place to lay low than here in the county of my birth? There were plenty of backwaters to hunker down in. I only needed to find one of my own. And I thought I knew where the best one would be.

The northeast corner of the county, not far from my burnt river cabin, runs into the tag ends of the Appalachians. The flats give way to rolling hills thick with woods and shot through with gullies and creeks and hollows. The canopies of the trees are thick, overhanging the roads, shading everything. Once you're in the midst of it, all points of reference are lost and clean lines of sight beyond twenty feet are hard to come by. Excellent terrain for laying low, for seeing without being seen. Not much had changed in these woods since before the Civil War and the people that lived scattered throughout these trackless miles enjoyed their arboreal seclusion and didn't welcome strangers.

Latoya drove while I directed her, trying as best I could to remember how to get there.

"These are some shit-ass scary woods," she said, looking around at the heavy cover of trees blocking out the sun.

"Some families went to ground here before the Civil War and haven't been heard from since," I said.

"Must be crazy crackers," she said, driving deeper and deeper down winding roads into the woods.

I tried to find the landmarks I'd navigated by the last time I'd been up this way.

"Up ahead," I said. "Turn up ahead just past that long-leaf pine that's hanging over the road."

"Long-leaf what?" she asked.

"There! Turn onto this dirt road here."

She turned right onto a narrow dirt track that left the main road. We moved deeper into the cover of the trees, the shade growing heavy.

"Just where are we going?" Latoya asked, leaning low over the steering wheel to peer ahead through the gloom.

"There's someone I know lives down this way," I said. "I'm thinking maybe he'll let me lay low for a few days until I decide what I'm gonna do next."

"What about me?" she asked.

I paused. "I haven't decided what I'm going to do about you," I said.

The dirt track ran uphill through switchbacks that the car could barely negotiate and finally settled out on a level spot. Through another thicket of trees we rolled into a clearing. A tin-roofed shack sat at the far end of the clearing, the yard around it holding a battered pickup.

"Stop here," I said.

She braked and we came to a stop at the edge of the clearing.

"This guy's a little jumpy," I said. "I want you to wait here while I go talk with him. Whatever you do, don't get out of the car."

I took the keys from the ignition and climbed out of the car, stuffing both pistols into my pants as best I could.

The sun was setting, sending shafts through the trees, casting the woods in a long golden light. The air hung cool, mixing with the smell of wood smoke. I felt suddenly chilly and a shiver ran through me. Keeping my hands in plain sight, I moved deliberately across the clearing toward the house.

A thick mat of pine straw and year-old fallen leaves littered the forest floor, crackling under my feet as I picked my way through the yard. Off to my right I heard a cluck and cackle, and made out a chicken coop behind the house. Farther to the right, trees had been cleared and a vegetable garden sat behind a six-foot deer fence. The shack itself was dark, though. No smoke rose from its chimney.

The old wooden steps leading up to the front porch

creaked underfoot, as if about to give way. The porch itself had settled badly, sagging away to the right. I stood for a moment on the porch, listening. Nothing but the squawk of blue jays and cardinals, and from somewhere far off a trickle of water. I knocked on the door.

I leaned to the left and peered through a window. The inside was dark. I knocked again.

"Clint!" I called. "Clint McConneyhead! It's Nelson Ingram. Are you there?"

Nothing.

I turned to look back at the car. Latoya sat sulking behind the wheel. The woods seemed to grow darker by the minute, though it couldn't have been past four o'clock.

A third knock on the door brought no answer. It was only as I turned and descended the steps back to the yard that I saw him. He stood in the lee of a large oak, the trunk between him and the car, dressed in worn camouflaged fatigues, a rifle in his hand. He had probably been standing there the whole time.

I smiled, but he held up a hand to silence me. He motioned for me to move toward him. As I approached, he pointed to the guns in my belt. I nodded and pulled each slowly out and tossed them aside on the ground.

After I had closed to within ten feet, he held up a hand. "That'll do right there," he said.

I stopped. "Hey, Clint," I said.

"Hey, Nelson," he said. "What brings you out this way?"

"Trouble," I said. "I'm kinda needing some help."

Clint lowered the rifle and looked from me to the sheriff's car. "I don't need no trouble, Nelson."

"I know, but I got nowhere else to turn. I just need a place to lay low for a couple of days until I can figure things out."

Clint flicked the safety on the gun and rested it against

the oak. He was the man who'd had words with Benny at The Rebel Yell yesterday over the merits of Hank Williams, Jr. He lived out here alone in the woods, holed up and hunkered down, still working out the ghosts of Vietnam. His only compromise with civilization was his monthly drive to the post office to pick up his VA and social security checks, and twice-weekly visits to The Rebel Yell to spend them. It was there that we'd passed more than one evening trading beers and stories.

He'd been a rifleman in an LRRP unit in the late sixties — Army Special Forces involved in long-range patrols behind enemy lines. The stories he would tell curled the hairs on my neck, but he intimated at much worse that he couldn't speak of. In '69, toward the end of his tour of duty, his unit had gotten pinned down in a firefight and had been cut to pieces. He'd held off the North Vietnamese while his sergeant got the dead and wounded to the landing zone to be choppered out. But Clint had been taken prisoner and had spent the next four years in a POW camp. They'd tortured him, given him TB and dysentery, but he'd held up, kept his mouth shut, and marked his time.

When he came home, he got his visit to the White House and five minutes of fame, was mustered out, then took his back pay and disability checks and disappeared into the Alabama woods that he'd known since he was a boy. Since then he'd bided his time in his little shack, seeking only quiet and anonymity. I'd run across him during long nights at the bar drinking away my own money. He sat nightlong at a corner of the room, sipping at his Bud and punching up Hank, Jr., Merle Haggard, and Willie Nelson on the jukebox. Only after months of pondering each other across the room did we finally start up a conversation across two tables.

He spent his days holding on tight, seeking quiet because he couldn't bear much else. But what had unmanned him was not the war, but having to come home from the war. What he couldn't stand was not the memory of what he'd been through, but the awful, endless, stupefying banality of life in America after the war. In our late nights over beer, when we talked about our lives now, he was awkward, monosyllabic, and nervous. But when he reminisced about the war, he lit up, words coming easily, his face growing animated as he recalled gallantry and great good humor in terrible times. Nothing that life had to offer afterward could compare. And whose fault was that?

Clint looked me in the face, then down at his feet. "Nelson," he said, "I really don't need no trouble."

I stood there, breathing hard suddenly, not knowing what to say. I had no right to be putting this on him, but had nowhere else to turn. I felt weak in the knees.

"You okay, Nelson?" Clint asked.

"I can't tell you half of what I've been through. I'm in such deep shit."

He reached out and grabbed my arm. "You need to come and sit down for a while? I can get you a glass of water."

"Thanks, Clint," I said.

"C'mon," he said, coming up beside me.

"There's someone else with me," I said, turning to look at the patrol car.

He nodded. "Can she wait there?"

"She might run off if I leave her alone."

"Would that be bad?"

"Kind of," I said. "She knows too much. More than I do, in fact."

He looked back at the car, clearly distressed. "Roger that," he said. "Bring her inside, but tell her she's got to behave."

"Thanks, Clint," I said.

He stood watching while I walked back to the car, picking up the pistols on the way. Latoya had rolled down the window of the car. She leaned out and looked at me, eyes wide.

"That's the big cracker who tried to pick a fight with us yesterday," she hissed. "What kinda shit are you getting me into?"

I opened the car door. "You better be quiet or that big cracker's gonna to lose his temper again," I whispered to her. "He's one of those nutso Vietnam vets likely go off over any little thing."

She climbed out. "I'll give him something to go off over," she said, pulling her arm away as I tried to take it.

I reached in and grabbed the knapsack. We walked together toward Clint, who still stood watching, a fretful look on his face, the rifle in the crook of his arm.

Latoya forced a big smile. "Howdy, y'all," she said. Then holding the smile, she whispered to me through clenched teeth, "This cracker's batshit crazy. Lookit how he's living out here. Lookit that goddamn gun he's toting."

"Behave," I whispered back.

We went with Clint up the steps. He stood at the door, looked at us, then down at his hands. Fumbling in his pocket, he pulled out a small ring of keys and unlocked the door. He hesitated, then opened it, and stood for a second in the doorway.

"Don't touch anything now," he said, seemingly embarrassed about letting others into his house.

We walked inside. Although the outside of the cabin was classic sepia-toned Southern Gothic, the inside was spare and pristine. The floorboards were scrubbed and clean, the walls whitewashed. A small kitchen in the corner was clean and squared away. A table and four chairs dominated the middle of the room. In the far corner was a single bed beside a bookshelf and a desk.

The room contrasted so strongly with his scraggly,

bedraggled appearance one had a moment's pause trying to reconcile the two. I made my way to the table and sat. Clint brought me a glass of water. It had an astonishingly clean taste to it.

"What's up with you, Nelson?" Clint asked.

Sitting down helped. "I'll be okay," I said. "Just let me sit here a minute."

"Sure," he said, looking from Latoya to me. She sat slumped at the table, staring sullenly out the front windows. Clint hovered uncertainly, casting his eyes about, worrying a dishtowel.

"Listen, Clint," I said, "I'm sorry to barge in on you like this, but I really have nowhere else to go."

"You gotta get rid of that cop car," Clint said. "Whoever it belongs to is gonna come looking for it, and I don't need that kind of trouble."

"Okay," I said. "Just give me a few minutes."

He pulled me up by the arm and took me back toward the front door.

"This is really not cool," he said, getting upset. "You can't be doing this." We were breaking into a sweat together, both of us breathing hard. "You gotta go."

I leaned against the wall, looking at him. I had no right to come into his space. He was jumpy enough just getting by day-to-day with nothing happening.

"I'm sorry, man," I started, then it all came out, "but the mob's after me and I don't know who all else. I got a money-laundering scheme of theirs busted last year and I stole a bunch of their money in the process and now they're trying to kill me. And it turns out I've got something else that they want too and I'm not even sure what it is and who wants it, and my cabin got burned down and William Charles is dead and Dr. Hartley's missing and the FBI's involved and I'm wondering if I can trust anybody and you were the only person I knew of who's so far off the map that nobody'd think to look here." I took a deep breath.

Clint stood there for a moment.

"I need a fucking joint," he said at last, shaking his head.

"First good thing I heard all goddamn day," Latoya said.

We sat again at the table. Clint took out a little box from a high cabinet in his kitchen and brought it over. Out of it he produced a zip-lock bag of marijuana and a pack of rolling papers. With practiced hands he rolled a joint as neat as any I'd seen, then lit up. He inhaled deeply, the ember at the end of the joint glowing, then passed it to me.

I took a polite toke, then passed it to Latoya, who snatched it from me hungrily.

"You wouldn't have any whiskey, would you, Clint?" I asked.

Alcohol, particularly Kentucky whiskey or bourbon, had always been my drug of choice. Its hot, smoky bite rolled around in the back of the throat, the pleasant little fire it kindled in the gut, the gentle way it eased you into a relaxed and contemplative state, were all cherished aspects of its pharmacopoeia. Last year I'd made a stab at sobriety for a few months, but finally had found life too harsh and miserly without the comforts of whiskey. Sadly but not surprisingly, bourbon's golden glow usually led to a lowered inhibition for a second drink, and a third and a fourth and I don't know how many more, followed by sodden nights and ragged mornings and afternoons in the grips of hangovers and shakes and acrimony and halfhearted vows to climb back on the wagon. Since my kidnapping by Benny and Latoya, I'd gone most of a day without a drink, though it felt like a year.

Clint served up three fingers of some kind of whiskey

in a smudged tumbler. He was firmly in the grip of his devil weed now and seemed far easier in his manner.

"Thank you," I said. "You don't know how much I need this."

"Sure," he said. He looked at Latoya, who had toked down more than half the joint and looked thoroughly shit-faced. "So," he said, "you want to tell me what this is all about?"

"Like I said, all these people are after me, some of them 'cause I ripped them off, but they also seem to be interested in this." I put the knapsack on the table and dumped the money and notebook out, then reached into my pocket and put the computer disks with them.

"I don't think it's the money they want," I said. I picked up the notebook and the floppies.

He took the notebook from me and thumbed through it.

"There's supposed to be account numbers to some Swiss bank accounts where a lot of money is stashed, but I looked through it last year and didn't see anything but a lot of sums and ledger entries."

"It's here," he said, flipping to the back. He showed me a page of numbers and letters.

"How can you tell?" I asked.

"Can't be sure, but it makes sense. This page is all scrambled. It looks like a cipher."

"What?"

"Encoded. A cryptogram." He looked intently at the page. "You might be able to get the bank names by doing a frequency analysis, but it could be in French or German or Italian or English, so it'd be hard. If the account numbers are encoded, though, you're really fucked. That'd be a bear to crack."

"How do you know all this?"

" 'Nam," he said. "I was in intelligence before I signed up for Special Forces. They teach you all sorts of shit." He picked up the floppies. Now that he had a problem in front of him, he seemed to be growing more comfortable in his own skin.

"I got no idea what's on those. Nobody knows I've got them."

"Until now," he said, looking at Latoya. "What's her story?"

We both looked at her. Stoned, she looked away and giggled.

"I saved her life last year," I said. "The mob was gonna kill her and I got her out of it and gave her most of the money I took from them, and to repay me she comes back with this asshole from L.A. and they both tried to rip me off."

"What do you know about these?" he asked her.

She looked down, fighting the giggles. "Not much. Just that they're worth some money. Maybe a lot."

The sunlight faded as the sun moved low in the west and the room was growing dim. We sat there for long minutes in silence as people under the influence can do.

"Okay," Clint said at last, standing. "Y'all can stay here until you figure this thing out. But first thing after it gets dark, we got to get rid of that cop car."

19

Hartley

W E drove by Demar's Bar, where the sheriff had been
tied up in the bathroom. Patrol cars had descended
upon it like flies on roadkill. We followed the highway out
into Colequit County for a good way, looking around and
listening on the police scanner. Halfway to the next county
we turned back and retraced our path. There was no sign of
Nelson. The day grew long, the sun sinking in the west,
and I was tired after the last two days. Finally, I said to the
colonel that we'd best call it a day and head in.

"Do you want to go back to my cabin?" he asked.

My back ached and my stomach grumbled. I hadn't
eaten for what seemed like days. "Sure," I said.

We drove down the back roads, avoiding Litchfield,
and rolled back up the dirt track to his cabin as dark fell.
It looked welcoming, as much like home as anyplace.
We walked up the steps, and he opened the door. I followed him, but he pulled up short in the doorway, bar-

ring my entry with his arms. Looking around him, I saw that the room held three men waiting on us, dressed in dark suits.

"Aureliano," one of them said—a short, dark fellow with an Elvis pompadour, "where have you been?" His accent was Latino.

"As you can see, I've been out," the colonel said. He lowered his arms and I edged into the room beside him.

The short dark fellow looked me up and down and raised his eyebrow—a thick furry line that ran all the way across.

"Excuse me," the colonel said, nodding in my direction. "May I introduce my friend, Dr. Seymour Hartley." He inclined he head toward the short fellow. "Dr. Hartley, this is Señor Esteban Mendoza."

Mendoza pulled himself up straight, took a step forward, and extended his hand. I met him halfway and we shook, his hand a meaty slab. "It is an honor, Dr. Hartley," he said.

"The honor is mine," I said, gratefully as he let go.

The other two men were similarly short and dark. They stood in echelon behind Mendoza, who had turned again from me to the colonel.

"It would seem that Señor Mendoza has something he wishes to discuss with us," the colonel said.

"Yes," Mendoza said. "I am here regarding your friend, Mr. Ingram."

"Seems like everybody's after Mr. Ingram," I said. "How do you know him?"

"From last year," he said. "We had an indirect interest in some of the ventures that he became ensnared in."

"Really?" I said.

Mendoza waved his hands. "No, you misunderstand. We were not involved with the *mafiosi*. We are freedom fighters exiled from Cuba." He puffed his chest out a bit and preened. "Castro has been for many years using Cuba as a transfer point for drug traffic from South America and he had some interest in the money-laundering operation that your friend uncovered. It is one of our tasks in the counterrevolution to monitor these activities and foil them when we could . . . by means not available to the police."

"We have contacts in law enforcement and in organized crime," Buendia put it. "After the arrests last year, there were rumors that money had been embezzled by the man directing the operation here. Quite a lot of money. But there were no accounts ever found and everyone down here had died violently. But we learned through our sources of yourself and Mr. Ingram."

I looked at the colonel. "So you retired here in the woods for the quiet?"

He looked down. "I came here to keep an eye on Mr. Ingram," he said, "and to find out what I could."

Mendoza stepped forward. "We need to know what you know."

"I know that you're a bunch of lying sons-of-bitches," I said.

The two men behind Mendoza came forward to flank him. Mendoza held up a hand to stay them. He looked at me sternly. "I am many things, many of them not so good, but I am not a liar."

We locked eyes for a long moment. He was a son-of-a-bitch. Maybe not a liar, or a very good one. There was steel there in this stocky little Cuban.

"I don't know much about it," I said. "Ingram got caught up in something he didn't understand. Lots of people got killed. He made off with some of their money. That's all I know."

"Where is the money?" Mendoza asked.

"I think he gave most of it away."

Mendoza looked at the colonel. "There was something else," he said.

"Might have been," I said, "but I don't know anything about it."

"We have information that there was something else. Account numbers for the money. And other . . . documents."

I sat down in a chair beside the door.

"Listen, boys," I said. "I have had one helluva last couple of days. My best friend's been killed, my house had been overrun with police, I've been shot at, left for dead, pulled out of the river, and run halfway across two counties on a wild-goose chase, and I am dog-tired. My back's killing me and I don't know anything else about what you want."

Mendoza sat down on the chair beside me. "Perhaps what you say is true," he said. "With so much money involved, it is hard to say."

"I, too, am a son-of-a-bitch," I said, "but not a liar."

He smiled. "No. I don't think that you are. Your friend Mr. Ingram may try to contact you, and his whereabouts are very important to us. I hope you understand if we keep you with us for the time being."

"No, I don't understand," I said, getting angry now. "All I understand is that the colonel here's been dealing with me under false pretenses, and the rest of you are only interested in laying your hands on some blood money, and I'd just as soon have nothing to do with the lot of you." I began to stand. "So, if you don't mind, I'm calling for a ride home."

Mendoza reached out a hand and pulled me back into my chair. For a fat man well past middle age, he was strong. He leaned into me, the aroma of sweat and cigars coming off him.

"Perhaps we can be of some assistance to you in exchange for your help here," he said.

I stared at him. Sitting down heavily in the chair had sent an ice pick of pain up my back. My eyes teared and muscle spasms crept up from my sacroiliac, but I held his gaze and did my best to show no outward distress.

"You seek those who killed your friend, yes?" he asked. His eyes were dull and riven with nets of blood vessels. His breath was an amalgam of stale and meaty odors. His skin was oily. He smiled and teeth glistened an off shade of yellow with one gold canine.

"Yes," I said evenly.

"But you do not know how to find these men, yes?"

I nodded.

"We can help you in this matter," he said.

"How is it that you know such men? I thought you were freedom fighters and these men were working with your enemy."

He smiled ruefully. "Would that matters were so simple. In our struggle against Castro, we have had to work outside the limits of the law. Outside of the limits of government. It makes for strange bedfellows. One day we might oppose them and the next we might use them for our own ends. It is the same with them. Perhaps it is the same with Fidel."

"You can tell me who these people are?"

He nodded. "I can bring them to you, if that is what you'd like."

I held out my hand and we shook. "I would like to see that," I said, "but if you lay a hand on Ingram or cause him to come to harm, then I'll do everything I can to stop you."

Mendoza smiled. "Very good." The men behind him relaxed visibly. The colonel shuffled his feet.

I stood up and looked at them all—old men, thick in the middle and slack in the neck, still fighting battles that were now over a quarter-century old, as if any amount of money would change the past, wipe away what they'd lost, and make them young again. I felt suddenly sad for them, while envying them their commitment. An old and hopeless cause might be better than what had taken up residence with me of late.

20

WE drove the sheriff's car out into the county. Latoya sat beside me and stared out into the dark.

"What are we gonna do?" she asked.

"When did this become 'we'?" I asked.

"Shit," she said, then sat in silence for a while.

I pulled over on the shoulder and rolled to a stop.

"This will do," I said.

We climbed out of the car and hunkered down along the edge of the woods. The evening was cooling off, the air still.

"What if that cracker doesn't show?" she asked after we'd sat for a few minutes.

"He'll show."

"Damn." She shivered and bent over, rocking herself.

"What am I going to do with you?" I asked her.

"Get that cracker to shoot me," she said.

Headlights topped the rise down the road, then the thrumming of the engine came to our ears.

"That's him," I said and edged back onto the shoulder.

The truck flashed its headlights and coasted to a stop on the shoulder behind the patrol car. Clint leaned over and popped open the passenger door. Latoya and I climbed inside and off we drove.

No one spoke for miles. Latoya sat between us, shivering and sniffling. Clint kept his eyes straight ahead as if he were trying to wish us away. A minute mart approached, its lights beckoning.

"You think we could get some beer?" I asked.

Clint's trance was broken and he turned to look at me, not comprehending for a moment. He blinked and looked ahead again. "Sure," he said at last.

It was a battered Quik-Stop with a pair of old gas pumps out front. We pulled into the parking lot. I opened the truck door. Latoya climbed out after me.

"I gotta make a phone call," she said.

"What?" I asked.

"A phone call," she said.

"You've got to be kidding."

"I need to call Little Reggie," she said, looking me straight in the eyes.

"A few hours ago you were willing to sell me out to L. Ron Hubbard, and now you want me to just let you drop dime to God-knows-who?"

"I need to call my Little Reggie," she said firmly.

I looked from her to Clint.

"He's in a foster home," she went on. "This is my day to call him. I can't miss it."

"I don't think so, man," Clint said.

She slammed the truck door. "I'm calling my kid," she said, "or I'm raising hell right here."

"Why should I trust you after all the shit you put me through?" I asked her.

"Dial the number. Listen in while I talk. I just need to call my baby." Her voice cracked.

"Okay," I said.

Clint shook his head, then looked the other way. Latoya and I walked to the pay phone that sat outside the store. She picked up the receiver and stared at it.

"I need some change," she said.

"C'mon," I said. We went inside the store together and I bought a six-pack of Bud and today's copy of the *Litchfield Ledger*, and then talked the clerk out of five dollars in quarters.

Back outside I watched her dial and drop most of the money into the phone. Holding my head close to hers, I listened as the phone rang and rang. We were almost cheek to cheek and her fragrance was in my nostrils—heady stuff after such a long couple of days. Ten rings, then fifteen must have passed. She held on to the receiver, waiting long beyond the time when anyone would have answered. Turning to look at her, I saw she was crying. Finally, after a couple of minutes and untold rings of the phone, she hung up the receiver.

"Maybe they were out," I said.

She wiped her eyes on the sleeve of her coat, then walked back to the truck. "Yeah," she said. "Let's go."

We drove the rest of the way back to Clint's cabin with little being spoken. When we got back, she strode rapidly away from the truck and went inside the cabin. Clint walked beside me, watching her.

"What's with her?" he asked.

"She's all messed up," I said. "I don't think she knows what side she's on."

We came to the steps of the porch. Clint sat slowly and looked out at the trees. I sat beside him.

"Sorry about dumping this on you," I said for the twentieth time.

"This is my favorite time of the day," he said, lighting up his second joint. "Quiet, starting to cool off."

"Yeah." I was finding it hard to get into the mellow, though. I felt as if I'd been beaten with a bat and dragged down the road.

"Can I get you another drink?" he asked.

"That might help," I said, grateful again.

He went inside and came back in a moment with two fingers of whiskey in a tumbler.

I'd opened the newspaper. The bank shooting was in a sidebar on page one, obviously pasted in at the last minute. At the end of the story it mentioned that Dr. Hartley had contacted the police.

"My friend, Dr. Hartley, is alive," I said. "He called the police this morning."

"Where is he?"

"It doesn't say," I said, leaning forward and peering at the print in the bare light from the windows.

"How'd you get yourself into all this shit?" he asked, sitting beside me again.

I sipped at the drink. "I don't know, Clint," I said. "One thing just led to another."

He handed me the joint. I took a small toke. "Do you grow this stuff?" I asked.

"So, this shit you got," he went on, ignoring the question, "why don't you just give it to the guys who want it?"

"I got a feeling they're not just going to settle for the notebook. I think my ass is part of the deal."

"You could run," he said.

"Ingrams don't run," I said, realizing the truth of it only after I'd said it.

He considered this a moment. "Be like water, man."

I looked at him quizzically.

"In 'Nam we had all the power, man. We could go where we wanted when we wanted. We could drive down any road like King Shit and rip the sky like God, and Victor Charlie still kicked our asses. Because when he needed to, he could flow quiet around us, silent as a creek, and when it served him, he could thunder like a waterfall. And he knew when to do each."

"I don't follow you," I said.

"Man, this is our backyard. We can set the terms. When we need to, we can seep into the forest like the night's dew and then we can thunder on their asses like Niagara Falls."

"If you say so."

"I don't go looking for trouble," Clint said, "but if trouble comes looking for me, it had better watch out."

I drained my glass and stood, picking up my six-pack of Bud.

"No doubt," I said, "and I'm grateful for your help, but I'm all in. I gotta bed down for the night."

He looked up at me. "The cots are inside. Do you mind if I look at the notebook and those disks?"

"Have at it," I said and went inside.

It was dark. Latoya had already gone to sleep in one the cots that Clint had laid out. I kicked off my shoes and pulled off my shirt. He'd laid out some sleeping bags on aluminum-frame canvas cots. I lay down on top of the sleeping bag. It felt better than sex to just lie down in the quiet. I let out a deep breath and felt two days' worth of stress unwind from my limbs. Clint came in a few minutes later and walked off to the corner. He turned on the lamp over the desk that sat beside his bed and I could see him flipping through the notebook.

I turned over and lay on my side. Latoya lay a few feet away. Her breath came evenly. I thought she was asleep. Then she said quietly, "So, what the fuck are we gonna do?"

She rolled over to look at me. In the half-light I could see little of her except those exquisite almond eyes. She sniffled and shivered and rubbed at her nose.

"You coming off the stuff?" I asked.

"Fuck you," she said.

"Why did you let Benny fuck you up like this?"

She lay for a long while staring at me in the dark. Finally she said, "I don't know. I was in the community college. I was gonna be an LPN. Then he showed up. Was all one big party after that. Before I knew it, I'd flunked out, Social Services took Little Reggie away, I was strung out on coke, and Benny was all I had left."

"So you decided to fuck me over?"

"He said there'd be a lot of money and that it'd be one way I could get myself out of trouble." She shivered again. "Oh, shit," she said in a little voice and started crying.

"Sorry," I said, not knowing what I was apologizing for.

"You shoulda just have let those greaseballs kill me. You shoulda just let me go back to L.A. and live my life. You shouldn't have given me that blood money. Nothing good coulda come of it. It's all been shit since then."

She was right. It had all been shit since I'd taken that money. It had poisoned everything, and nothing had been right since.

"We'll make it right," I said.

"Heard that story before," she said.

So had I.

That's what I'd said to my father in Washington. We'd gone to the Smithsonian and Jefferson Memorial that day. He'd been nipping at his hip flask the whole time. Toward the end of the day, we'd climbed the steps to the Lincoln Memorial. He'd stood with me looking up at the mammoth statue, one of my father's heroes. The whiskey showed itself in the heaviness of his gait and the deliberateness of his movements. He looked from the monument across to the green lawns of the mall and the Washington Monument. In turning he stumbled, dropped down a step, then fell. He sprawled in front of Lincoln, drunk.

I had come to his side. He looked from me to the statue and back at me. He flushed, humiliated. Suddenly our roles were reversed. I helped him to his feet.

"It's okay, Dad," I'd said. "Let's get up. We'll make it right."

He stood and looked around and I saw in his eyes such confusion. He looked down at me.

"Sure," he said.

21

THE Flying Burrito Brothers departed the cabin, leaving the colonel and me alone again. He heated a can of soup on his stove and we ate it sitting across from each other at his kitchen table. There wasn't much said. He couldn't bring himself to look me in the eye.

Finally he said, "I am sorry."

"Bullshit you're sorry," I said. "You lied to me and played me for a fool."

"Necessity has its dictates," he said. He looked down into his soup like he was contemplating the bottom of the ocean.

"That's what your hero Castro would have said. Or Stalin."

He sighed. "I am sorry," he said again. "Life is long and the decisions we make put us into some strange places. I respect you as a man and regret the situation into which events placed us."

"Who are these men?"

"Disenfranchised aristocrats from Cuba, and the sons of disenfranchised aristocrats. Their families fled to Florida after Castro and they grew up with their fathers' dreams and hatreds. Their fathers died and they assumed their roles in their new businesses and the old hatreds. And now they, too, are old and they hold on to their hatreds as the only constants in their lives across the years."

"And that doesn't describe you?"

He smiled faintly. "I don't think so. I have my own agenda with Castro, but I am no son of the aristocracy. I really did run a liquor store in Tampa."

"Then why are you with them?"

"Some favors were owed from the past."

"Can I trust them?"

"You can trust them to do what is in their own best interests and to keep their word if it doesn't conflict too strongly with those interests."

I shook my head. "I'm tired. I need to lie down. Can you drive me home?"

"I don't think it would be a good idea for you to go back to that house. You are too much of a target there. You can stay here again tonight. It will be safer."

I stood. Pain, my old friend, greeted me. "Can I use the same bed?"

He nodded. "Of course."

"Thank you."

"I am sorry, Seymour," he said.

I turned to him. "That's okay. But lie to me again and I'll kill you."

"To live is to lie," he said, "to oneself and others."

22

WHEN I awoke, it was still dark, except for the glow that came from Clint's desk. I rolled over and looked in that direction. He still sat at the desk working. Climbing off the cot, I walked over to him. He was using a computer that had sat away in a corner of the desk.

"Hey," he said.

"What time is it?" I asked.

"About five."

"You been working all night?"

"Pretty much."

"Found anything?"

"The stuff at the back of the notebook is definitely a substitution cipher. But like I said, if it's just bank names and account numbers, then it's gonna be pretty much impossible to break without the key."

"Yeah," I said, "so it's hopeless, right?"

"Well, I started looking at these floppy disks you had."

"Jeez, I was surprised you had electricity. Where'd you get the computer?"

"Built it from a kit. Got a 386 chip. Eight megs of RAM. So, I put these disks in. There's a bunch of text files on them. Like hundreds of pages."

"Text files?"

He typed in a command and called one of them up into a text editor.

"Yeah," he said, "like some guy's memoirs. Some wild shit. But I did a search through the text looking for long strings of numbers and I turned up this."

He scrolled down through this long text file until in the middle of it he came across a couple of lines of letters and numbers. The first line was letters *a* through *z* and then the numbers *0* through *9*. On the second line was a different set of letters and numbers lined up under the top one.

I looked at him.

"It's the key, man," he said. He pointed to a slip of paper where he'd used it to go through the cipher from the notebook. It spelled out the names of four banks in French followed by what looked like account numbers.

"Shit," I said.

"Swiss account numbers, man," he said. "Numbered accounts. We just gotta show up with these numbers and take the money."

"No shit?"

He giggled, stoned still after a long night of work. "I don't know, man. But I cracked the code. Everyone wouldn't be after it if you couldn't use this to get the money."

He shut down the computer. "I gotta rack up some sack time," he said and fell into his bed.

In a minute he was snoring. I looked at the piece of paper where he'd cracked the code, then folded it up and put it in my pocket. Latoya slept in the cot beside mine. I stepped out onto the front porch.

Still dark outside, the air hung cold around me. A predawn quiet reigned. I sat on the front steps. All my muscles ached. My head pounded from the night of whiskey and pot and restless sleep. What was I going to do? I was sitting on top of untold millions with my life at stake and God-knows-who on my trail. I didn't know where the police and the FBI fell out in all this and who I could trust. I held a few cards, but still didn't understand the rules of the game.

I feel like I needed advice, but didn't know who to turn to. I needed to contact Hartley in the morning.

BOOK 3

To live outside the law, you must be honest.

—Bob Dylan,
"Absolutely Sweet Marie"

23

WE sat in Buendia's pickup outside The Rebel Yell, waiting. The day had warmed up, and sitting in the truck, I broke a little sweat. This felt good after the night before. I was running short on my morphine tablets, so was husbanding them. I tossed and turned and ached. Now in the modest heat of this late afternoon I felt a little better.

After a bad night and a bad breakfast, I'd called my home answering machine to check for messages. Aside from a few calls from the police wondering where I was and asking me come in for "a few questions," there was nothing. Then I had called my office at the hospital. The secretary said that somebody had just dropped off an envelope for me. "A tall, wild-looking fellow with long hair and a beard. Smelled like last year's sweat socks," she said.

The colonel and I had driven in to pick it up, coming

and going as quickly as we could. The envelope contained a handwritten note from Nelson:

> I'm alive and more or less in one piece and hope this note finds you the same. I read in yesterday's paper that you were alive but your whereabouts were unknown. As usual, I'm in a spot and need some advice. If you can, I'd like to meet. I'll be in The Rebel Yell, down the road from my (ex-) cabin at 7 every night this week on the chance you'll get this and show.

Typical Ingram. I wasn't sure why I was doing this. Something about revenge, as I recalled. Shit. Revenge was the emptiest of motives. When Andrew, my son, had been lost in Vietnam, I had looked for something to take my anger out on, but there was nothing handy. Lacy said I never was the same after he died and I couldn't disagree with her. But then, she should see me now. With her gone too, and William murdered, I was nothing but a shriveled-up, cancer-ridden bastard hell-bent to take it out on someone. On God, if I could find Him, but on anyone else if it came to that. And the list was growing longer by the day.

"Okay," I said to the colonel, "I'm going inside. Give me about ten minutes, then come in behind me and take a seat by the door."

He nodded. His Cuban friends had so far not shown their faces today and he hadn't had any opportunity I had seen to talk with them, so I was hoping that I'd be able to pull this meeting off undisturbed.

I climbed out of the truck. Outside of the closed cab, the air was cool, the autumn sun weak. The pain in my back bit for a moment then settled down and I walked into the bar.

It wasn't much to look at inside—Stars 'n' Bars and

NASCAR photos on the walls, plain tables and chairs scattered across the room, country music on the jukebox. The bartender was a down-home sort. He eyeballed me and nodded a cursory "hey" my way. A crowd filled the place as the after-work business had reached its peak. Nelson was at least smart enough to know there was relative safety in numbers.

I saw him in the far corner, sitting against the wall. He raised his chin and then his glass in my direction as I made my way between the tables toward him. Off to his right against the other wall sat a rangy, bearded, wild-looking fellow pretending to look the other way. I wondered if this was the one who'd delivered the envelope this morning, now covering Nelson's flank. The boy may have learned something in the last year.

I sat opposite him at the table. He had an extra glass waiting and poured me a beer from the pitcher at the table.

"Thanks for coming," he said. He looked like hell—pale and drawn and unwashed. About like I felt.

"No problem," I said.

"I didn't know if you were alive until I saw the newspaper," he said.

"What about you?" I asked. I took a drink of the beer.

He shook his head. "Long, strange trip." Then he told me what happened since he'd driven off night before last: coming back and finding the cabin burning, getting shanghaied by that California son-of-a-bitch, a shootout in front of the bank, escape in the Mercedes, betrayal by the black woman, the second shootout at the bar and grill, then escape again, and now lying low out in the country. It sounded like pulp fiction.

"Another Ingram mess," I said.

He smiled sheepishly and sipped at his beer, then told me about the notebook and the account numbers and all the money that might be there and how this was what everyone seemed to be after. Then I told him about my end of things—the hit man at the cabin, the interrogation, throwing myself into the river, washing up downstream, the colonel, the Cubans.

"So," he said, "it's the Cubans and the Florida mob who're after this?"

"Where is this little notebook?" I asked.

"In a safe place," he said.

"Is this who's covering your flank?" I asked, nodding my head toward the good-ol'-boy.

The good-ol'-boy met my eyes then looked away, nervous and irritable as a live wire.

"Yeah," Nelson said. "Clint McConneyhead."

I thought he looked like a McConneyhead—skinny, chinless, lank-haired men with rounded receding foreheads and milky blue eyes. A long line of them had been squatting out in the backwoods around here for five generations. As I recalled, they had a family history of colon cancer. I'd read the pathology slides on at least a dozen McConneyheads, McKonnieheds, MacConnyheads, and the like over the years. He turned to look at me again and then looked away. This one seemed wound very tight.

"So what are we going to do?" Nelson asked.

"What do you mean "we," paleface?" I asked and laughed. "You're the one in the crosshairs."

"You're in this, too. Like it or not."

He was right about that. "You've got what they all want. At least some of the folk involved want your ass in the bargain. If you don't want the money, perhaps you could work out a trade that would get you off the chopping block."

"Wouldn't know where to start," he said.

"These Cubans. Perhaps they could be of use," I said.

"Do you trust them?" he asked.

"I don't trust anyone. But maybe they could be of use."

He drank deeply from his beer. "I don't know. Maybe I should just turn it over to the FBI."

"Sure," I said. "Witness protection program. In six months you could be named Wilson and selling used cars in Provo. They'd get me a slot in Sun City."

He drained the glass. "The hell with it," he said. "Let's see what the Cubans can do for us."

24

HARTLEY looked like hell—gaunt and pale and worn. He moved stiffly and sat forward on the edge of his seat as if he were uncomfortable. But I was happy to see him after the past couple of days not being sure if he was even alive.

He didn't seem much in the mood for pleasantries. From the story he told, he'd been through his share of trouble since we'd parted. Finally, I had to ask him for help like I had before. I hated it, but he was in it with me.

Of course, he looked at me without flinching and said, "I'm on board."

"You okay, Seymour?" I asked.

He nodded. "Tired," he said.

"I can only guess," I said.

"Tired of it all. Tired of living."

"We could just run," I said.

"Sure," he said. "Witness protection. In six months you

could be named Wilson and selling used cars in Provo. They'd get me a slot in Sun City." He raised his glass and drank deeply from it.

"So these Cubans," I asked, "how could they help us?"

"I don't know," he said, "but it wouldn't hurt to listen."

"Do you trust them?"

"Don't trust anyone," he said.

"Okay," I said. "Let's see what they can do for us."

He turned in his chair and scanned the room behind him. A man stood and came toward us.

"Who's this?" I asked.

"One of my Cubans," he said.

He sat down—a balding, dark-skinned older man with a roman nose and piercing brown eyes.

"This is Señor Buendia," Hartley said.

His handshake was firm. "Mr. Ingram," he said, "it is a pleasure to finally meet you."

"Mr. Buendia has been living beside you for the last year," Hartley said.

"Really?" I asked. Was this the dark fellow on the neighboring lot? "What for?"

"You know what for," he said.

I looked away.

"There were things you took," he said.

I nodded.

"More than just cash?"

"I've just found out about it," I said.

"Account numbers?" he asked. "And other information?"

I nodded.

"You have problems perhaps I can help you with," he said. "Because of these things, people are looking to harm you. They've already killed Dr. Hartley's friend and seek him as well. I have contacts who can intercede on your behalf. In exchange for the items you still hold."

"That information may be worth a lot of money," I said. "What's your interest in it?"

He smiled. "A finder's fee, perhaps. But that is my business."

"Why don't I just keep it for myself?"

"Because then our friends would still be after you. And they are relentless. Besides, I doubt you will be able make any use of this information. I would imagine we are talking about bank account numbers. Perhaps numbered Swiss accounts. It will take expertise to access these accounts. You cannot simply call up on the phone and expect to withdraw the money."

I looked at Hartley. "What do you think?" I asked.

He shrugged. "You're not exactly in a strong position," he said. "I don't know what else to do to help you."

"How would you proceed?" I asked Buendia.

"We would need to see this information," he said, "to verify its worth."

"What guarantees do I have?"

"Only my word," he said.

Hartley laughed. "And he's been lying to me most of the last two days."

"They were only necessary lies. but now I give you my word that I will protect your interests and only proceed with your consent."

"When do you want to do this?"

"Whenever is convenient for you, but I would not wait long. I think our opportunity for negotiations is only a brief one."

My stomach rumbled and sank. I needed to make a decision. "Later tonight? Where shall we meet?"

"I can arrange a meeting at my cabin in a couple of hours."

I looked at Hartley again. He looked back at me. I could

see he didn't have much left. It was time to try to cut our losses and get out with our skins.

"Okay," I said. "I'll be there."

Buendia smiled. "I think you are making the right choice." He stood. "We will be expecting you."

Hartley stood slowly, Buendia standing with him. With a nod, they turned and left.

Clint looked over. He shook his head. We both watched them leave then scanned the room to see if anyone followed. Clint held a book of matches in his hands. The matches had all been lit and burned and piled onto the table. Beside that, a small pile of paper napkins has been twisted and shredded.

"Bad shit," he said.

He moved over and took an empty chair at my table. "You're gonna be lucky to get out of this alive," he said.

We waited for about ten more minutes, sipping at the beer, then I said, "We need to get moving."

Clint stood. "I'll check out back," he said.

He headed out the back door of the bar. I sat there and scanned the room again to see if anyone moved to follow. It seemed paranoid, but after the last few days, no precaution seemed too extreme. After a few minutes, I followed him out back.

He stood outside the back door beside the dumpster. He'd stashed an AR-15 behind it, and now held it against his thigh. Together we headed into the woods behind the bar. He let me lead and covered my rear, watching the back door of the bar. Twenty yards into the trees we stopped and listened. He squatted low and peered through the trees.

After a few long minutes had passed with nothing stirring, he stood. "Let's go," he said.

It was about a ten-minute hike through the woods to where he'd left his truck along an old logging road. Only after we'd gotten there, as we climbed into the pickup, did he say quietly, "Shouldn't have told him who I was."

I looked at him. "Jeez. Didn't think about it."

"Just better hope they don't know where I live," he said.

We climbed into the truck. I felt suddenly exposed again and stupid. The last thing I had wanted to do was place Clint at risk.

"Shit," I said.

He laid the rifle along the floorboards and cranked the engine. "Water under the bridge."

Pushing in the cigarette lighter on the dash, he fished out a joint from his shirt pocket.

25

THE Cubans were waiting for us when we got back to the cabin, this time without the subtlety of parking their car out of sight. Night had fallen and once again a chill settled, bringing out all my aches and pains. As the colonel and I walked up the steps and inside, I asked him, "You're vouching for these banditos, aren't you?"

"As much as I can vouch for anybody," he said grimly.

One of them sat on the front porch, keeping watch, a shotgun across his lap. He nodded to us as we passed by.

Inside, the other two sat at the kitchen table in dim incandescent light, the smell of cigars heavy in the air, watching us silently as we came in. Mendoza rolled a tumbler of rum between his hands, looking at the colonel expectantly.

"Ingram is coming," the colonel said. "In about an hour."

"Very good," Mendoza said.

"He's under the impression that you can help him with the dilemma he's in," I said. "That you can get the mob off his back."

Mendoza smiled broadly.

"Can you?" I asked.

"We shall see," he said.

"Well, he's going to want to hear more than that. And so will I."

He sipped at his drink. "I have made some calls. They are willing to bargain but want assurances that Ingram has what they want."

"He will be bringing that tonight," the colonel said.

"Then we shall see. If Mr. Ingram has what they want, then perhaps a deal can be arranged."

"Where does that leave me?" I asked.

Mendoza poured me a drink. "My good doctor," he said, "I have not forgotten you. The man who killed your friend is already dead. He was killed during the raid on Ingram's cabin."

"I don't want him. I want the men behind it all," I said. I sat down with him at the table and picked up the rum. It bit and burned going down—a most uncivilized drink appropriate to the circumstances.

"Who do you want, then?" Mendoza asked.

"The one in charge. The man who gave the orders."

. He reflected for a moment. "That is a very difficult task."

"Try," I said.

He pursed his lip. "Old Man Trafficante is gone. Died last year. Everything is up in the air."

"What are you saying? No one is in charge?"

"It is difficult to say. But their interest here is strong. The people who we will be dealing with will be the ones in authority."

"They'll be here?"

"He is here. He is most concerned with how badly things have gone. Frank Losurdo. I spoke with him last night."

"What did you tell him?" the colonel asked.

"Only what he needed to know," he said. "That we have information that he wants, and we may be able to work out mutually beneficial arrangements."

"You know," the colonel said to me, "it will be difficult to work out a bargain that spares Mr. Ingram if you then try to kill these men. They will not be likely to take it well."

Mendoza waved a hand. "Leave revenge to later," he said. "It is a dish that is best served cold and with age. It is enough for now that you will meet these men and look them in the eye. Later I will tell you where to find them."

He jabbed his big Cuban cigar into his mouth and smiled broadly, his face swart and oily in the dim light. Raising his rum, he offered a toast, "To mutually beneficial arrangements."

I raised my glass and met his. We drank. It burned all the way down.

26

Ingram

CLINT and I drove down toward my burned cabin. We had both the windows rolled down and the cool night blew by us. As we drew closer, I told him to pull up short of my property onto the shoulder. He rolled to a stop along the side of the road and killed the engine and lights. We sat for a moment, both of us listening. Nothing but the muted rustle of the woods came to our ears.

"Listen," I said to Clint, "I can take it from here. You've done more than you should. Why don't you just drop me off and head home. If you don't hear from me, you can drop Latoya off back in town tomorrow."

Clint sat there for a moment. "It's okay," he said at last. "I'll go with you and lay back in the woods while you go inside."

"This isn't your battle."

"*Semper fi,* man. I'm there."

"That's the Marine Corps," I said. "I thought you were with the Rangers."

"Yeah, but the Corps always had better propaganda. Just let me cover your ass. I can do this kind of shit really good. Only thing I was ever any good at."

I shook my head. "Thanks. I hope I don't need you."

We climbed out of the truck. Clint reached behind the seat and pulled out two AR-15s and handed me one. He paused and we listened again for a moment.

"Which way?" he asked.

I headed straight into the trees and Clint followed. We walked single file. This was the property upriver from my cabin. I'd told Clint to pull off the road well short of my land so we could approach the Cuban's cabin hopefully unobserved. The tract was woods along the roadway and bottom land along the river that flooded every spring. I cut diagonally across it. After about five minutes of carefully picking through the trees, we came to my fence line.

I was breathing hard and my leg ached where I'd been shot last year. We stood close to the place where the hit men had crossed onto my property a few nights ago. I picked my way carefully over the fence, avoiding the barbed wire strand that ran across the top. But I caught my trailing toe and fell to the ground on the far side. I grunted as I hit the dirt. The rifle clattered to the ground beside me.

"Shit," I whispered, lying there hoping I hadn't been heard by anyone.

"You okay?" Clint hissed at me.

"Yeah," I whispered back. I rolled to my side and stood. Clint came over the fence cleanly.

I picked up the rifle and we headed across my property. We came to the burnt remains of my cabin. Beside it stood my old LTD, scorched with its tires blown. The smell of cinders hung in the air. My patrimony, all that remained of my father and the ragged Ingram legacy, was here. I had failed to sire any heirs and had lost all that had been left to me, and now here I was in the midst of another foolhardy quest that would surely do little but add to the ruin.

"You weren't kidding," Clint said, surveying the scene.

"Spilt milk," I said, mustering as much false courage as I could. I headed toward the far property line.

The fence here was down in a couple of spots and I picked my way over. Across the Georgia-Pacific tract I could see the Cuban's cabin, its lights on, smoke coming from its chimney.

"You stick here," I said to Clint.

He nodded, staring through the trees at the cabin, fidgeting from foot to foot.

"You okay?" I asked. "You can always head out if you don't like things."

"No, I'm cool," he said. "Just kinda gets juices flowing that haven't run in a long time. Know what I mean?"

I nodded. "Yeah," I said, too familiar with such juices lately. I turned and began to make my way slowly toward the cabin.

About twenty yards short of the cabin, the woods gave way to a clearing. I stopped and knelt beside the trunk of an old oak. The cabin was a tin-roofed shack mounted only on cinderblocks. The air was dry and cold, the night still. I could feel my pulse hammering away in my neck, the ache and fatigue in all of my muscles. I didn't have the stomach for what I had to do next. How had I come to this again?

Beside the cabin, a car and truck were parked. I could see the silhouette of someone standing on the front porch with the occasional red glow of a cigarette.

I stood and walked out into the clearing, pausing for a moment to see if there was any response. When nothing happened, I headed toward the cabin. I stopped again at the foot of the steps. The shadowy figure on the porch moved to put himself between me and the front door. He carried a shotgun, raising it from his hip to point at me.

I kept my rifle pointed at the ground and held my other hand up. "I'm here to meet with your friends," I said.

"Ingram?" he asked in a deep, Latin-accented voice.

"Yes."

"You must leave the gun outside."

"I don't think so," I said.

He held his gun on me. "I have my instructions," he said.

"Well, I've got mine, too. If your people want to talk with me, it's on my terms."

He stood there for a moment longer, then opened the front door and stuck his head inside. He said something in Spanish and more Spanish came back from the room. The door swung and the man waved me inside. In the light from the room I could see that he was a middle-aged Latino fellow with a care-worn face lined like an East Coast road map. Beyond him, in the room, I could see other men gathered around a table.

I walked past the first Cuban. He eyed me coolly, then stepped inside, closing the door and leaning against it with his shotgun still on me. I stood between him and the table feeling trapped. Moving out of the center of the room, I edged toward an empty corner, fingering the safety on my rifle.

At the table sat Hartley, Buendia, and two other Latinos. Between them sat a bottle of Bacardi and three cigars smoldering in ashtrays.

One of the Latinos stood and extended a hand. "Good evening, Mr. Ingram. I am Señor Esteban Mendoza. I believe you have already met Señor Buendia."

I nodded toward them, shifted my rifle to my left, and shook Mendoza's hand. The unnamed man at the table eyed me flatly, saying nothing.

"Sit, please," Mendoza said, gesturing toward the table.

The unnamed fellow stood, yielding his chair to me with the same flat stare.

His chair put me with my back to the man guarding the door—a position that made me uncomfortable. I sat reluctantly, shifting the chair around so that I could watch the fellow with the shotgun out of the corner of my eye.

"It's still not clear to me how you can be of assistance to me," I said. I laid the AR-15 across my lap. My mouth was dry and the bottle of Bacardi called to me. Buendia picked up on it immediately, and rose to get a clean tumbler from a cupboard. He placed it on the table in front of me and poured a generous dollop of rum. While hardly my liquor of choice, it went down well, seeming to rinse my mouth clean of the grime of days, burning cozily in my stomach.

"My associates and myself are members of the anti-Castro resistance," Mendoza began. "Over the years we have acquired many contacts—a network for obtaining information about the operations of Castro in Cuba and in this country. For years we have known that Castro was instrumental in the trafficking of cocaine into your country. This has provided him with access to dollars, and I am sure he believes that in doing so he helps to undermine your culture. Santos Trafficante in Tampa was a principal associate here. After the fall of Batista, Lansky and all the other mobsters left Havana. But Trafficante stayed behind. Castro imprisoned him, and he could have easily had him executed with all the others sent to the wall in those days. Instead, he set him free and allowed him to return to America. It doesn't take a genius to see that deals were made.

"Trafficante's people set up the money-laundering operation that you stumbled upon last year. Many people are in jail and many people are dead, and Trafficante's people want revenge upon you and Dr. Hartley for your part in it."

"I think I know most of this," I said.

"Context is everything," Mendoza said. "Nothing has meaning without context. It had long been suspected that the man running the laundering at the embarkation point here had been skimming off the top. There was no word about this from or within the FBI, but the rumors ran strong. When your identity was learned, it was natural that they would seek you out both for revenge and to find out what you knew about this latter topic."

"I still don't see how you fit in," I said.

"You have something that these mobsters want badly. They would be willing to exchange the contract they've taken out on you and Dr. Hartley for this information. We have contacts with them and could perhaps use our position as a go-between for a finder's fee."

"And why should I give up all that money?" I asked.

"It won't do you much good if you're dead," Buendia said.

"So, may we inspect this information?" Mendoza asked. "If I am to vouch for its worth, I need to satisfy myself first of its veracity."

I pulled a Xerox of the critical page from the ledger from an inside pocket of my coat, unfolding it and laying it in front of them. Mendoza picked it up and inspected it.

"What is this?" he asked.

"It's a substitution cipher," I said. "It encodes bank names and account numbers. Swiss bank accounts."

"How do you know this?"

"Because I have the encryption key and I've decoded it."

"And I suppose that you didn't bring that key with you?"

"My days as a trusting fellow are long past. It's my insurance. You show this to our mob friends. They'll never break the code without the key. I'll provide them with the key in exchange for a million dollars in small bills and guarantee of safety for myself and Dr. Hartley. They'll be given copies of everything. The originals of all this will be retained by myself in a safe-deposit box at an undisclosed location, to be turned over to the FBI in the event of my demise."

Buendia took the paper from Mendoza and inspected it. "Where was the encryption key?"

"Hidden within some other materials I took last year."

"Other materials?"

"Files."

He considered this. Mendoza took the sheet from him, saying, "We will take this offer to them. But be prepared to take less."

"We'll see," I said. I had a moment of hope that things might work out after all.

A crash came off to my left. The door flew open and the Cuban with the shotgun stumbled to the floor. A man stood in the open doorway. He walked into the room and another followed him. I grabbed the AR-15 and thumbed off the safety. The Latino who stood behind me stepped forward, putting himself between the door and the table. The one on the floor rolled to bring the shotgun to bear. The first man took a step forward and kicked the shotgun away, while the second one strode into the center of the room holding a MAC-10 close to his side.

Mendoza stood and held up his hands. "Stop!" he said. "No shooting!"

Everyone stood still for a moment, giving Mendoza a chance to move to the center of the room.

"These are the associates I was telling you about," he said. He walked up to the two men who had come through the door. "You were not to have come here," he said.

"The boss got itchy," the first one said. "He wanted to

see the goods for himself." He had a Northeast accent—
Philadelphia or New Jersey.

"This is not the proper time or place," Mendoza said.

Just then, a third man walked into the room.

"Señor Losurdo," Mendoza said.

The man took Mendoza's hand and shook it.

"I couldn't wait, Esteban," he said. "I had to see for myself." He was a compact man with boot-blacked hair
combed straight back off his forehead and a pockmarked
face. He wore an expensive-looking suit of gray silk.

"This is not what was agreed upon," Mendoza said.

"Things change," he said. His eyes were dark and as
cold as a reptile's. He nodded at one of his men. "Keep an
eye outside while I talk with these fellows."

The man slipped outside, while the other kept his machine pistol trained in our direction.

"Is this Ingram?" he asked, inclining his head in my direction.

Mendoza interposed himself between us. "Please," he
said, "we will share all that we know in good time."

"And that time is now," he said, pushing past Mendoza.
He stood over me. "You're Ingram, aren't you?"

I stood, holding my rifle at my side. "Yes," I said.

He smiled—a grimace that bared his canines like a
wolf. "Man, but you have been a hair up my ass." He patted me heavily on the cheek. "You little prick . . ."

I took a step back. "I'm a big prick," I said, bringing the
rifle up between us, "and you assholes have been a hair up
my ass for the last year, too. I didn't go looking for your
bullshit."

He grabbed the muzzle of the rifle and held it down toward the floor, then pulled me close again by yanking at
the gun. "You wouldn't have had to put up with my shit if
I woulda known who you were sooner," he said. "Now
what you gotta do is give me a good reason not to bury a

cap in your head right now. I got issues with you and killing you would help me work through things real good."

He pushed me back again and wrenched the rifle from my hands as I stumbled backward. I fell against the wall of the cabin and caught myself. He tossed the rifle onto the kitchen table.

"So," he went on, "you need to give me one good reason why I don't kill you right here." He turned and coughed thickly, producing a handkerchief from a pocket.

Buendia picked up the photocopy from the table and handed it to Losurdo. He snatched it from him and looked at it, tipping it back and forth in the dim light.

"What the fuck is this alphabet soup?" he asked.

"Account numbers," I said.

"My ass," he said.

"It's encrypted," I said.

He tossed the paper back onto the table. "And I got this bridge in Brooklyn for sale."

"I have the encryption key," I said. "It decodes into bank names and account numbers for five numbered Swiss accounts."

He looked at me, seeming to take me seriously for the first time. "Show me," he said.

I laughed at him—a nervous explosion that made me feel sick, like the yap of a hyena. "Then you'd kill me for sure. That key is the only thing keeping me alive."

He picked up the photocopy again and folded it and stuffed it in his coat pocket.

"You won't be able to decode it without the key," I said.

"So what do you want?" he asked. He coughed again, spitting into his handkerchief.

"Guarantees of my safety as well as Dr. Hartley here. A million dollars in small bills. I'll give you copies of everything. I'll keep the originals in a safe-deposit box. They'll be turned over to the FBI if I meet an unnatural end."

He looked from me to the others.

"Okay," he said, "but I'll want some guarantees." He turned to his lieutenant. "Take the old man."

"Which one?" he asked.

"The skinny one — Hartley."

Buendia stood. "No. He is ill and in pain. I will go with you."

Hartley stood beside him. "I'm fine," he said. "I'll go."

"You don't need hostages," I said. "I'll bring the material here tomorrow."

Losurdo took Hartley and ushered him into the arms of his lieutenant. Hartley went willingly.

"We'll be back here tomorrow at the same time," he said. "If you have what I want, I'll let you and the old man live."

They pulled open the door. Losurdo moved out onto the porch. His lieutenant backed out after him. In a moment they were gone.

Mendoza looked at me.

"I am sorry," he said. "I did not anticipate this. They must have followed us back here."

"I thought you knew how to handle these guys," I said.

"We do," he said. "You will have to trust me."

"So far, that hasn't been working too good for me."

Buendia came to my side. "You must bring the key tomorrow. You will have to trust us to handle these men."

I picked up my rifle from the table. The other Cubans shifted around on their feet, clearly embarrassed at having been caught flat-footed by the mobsters.

"I'll let you know in the morning," I said and headed out the door.

27

Hartley

WELL, this was an interesting development. The greaseballs were taking me with them, thinking that I gave a goddamn about whether I lived or died. As long as I could be sure I'd find them already in hell when I got there, the precise timing of my death didn't concern me too much. I walked with them out of the cabin and back to their car—a Lincoln Towncar.

"In the back, Grandpa," one of them said.

I pulled my arm free of him. "I ain't your grandpa, sonny," I said, opening the door and sitting down.

Losurdo got into the backseat beside me while the two junior greaseballs climbed into the front.

"So, Gramps," Losurdo said, "I should kill you right now."

"And I should kill you, too, Guido," I said.

He laughed, then coughed heavily. "A couple of my men are dead because of you. And that's just this year."

"And my best friend is dead because of you," I said.

He coughed again then lit a cigarette. "Maybe that makes us even." In the flare from his lighter, his face looked drawn. It was then that I noticed that his collar gapped loosely around his neck, as if he had lost weight.

We set off from the colonel's cabin, bumping down the road and onto the highway.

"Where are you taking me?" I asked.

"This asshole Ingram," he went on, "he for real?"

"As real as Ingrams get these days."

"You better hope he comes through with the goods," he said, "or you'll be sleeping with the catfish."

The goombahs in the front seat laughed. "That's good," the driver said.

"He'll come through," I said. "Noble sacrifice is his specialty."

"A choirboy?" Losurdo asked.

"There's something to be said for that," I said.

We drove in silence for a long while, making our way through Litchfield and into the county beyond. Ten minutes later, we pulled up to a trailer on a lot just off Highway 74.

Inside was spartan—a couple of chairs and an old sofa around a television propped on a crate. They herded me in and the two goons promptly occupied the sofa, leaving me standing in the middle of the room. One lieutenant switched on the TV while the other lit up a cigarette and kicked off his shoes.

"Sit down, Gramps," Losurdo said.

I pulled one of the chairs over and sat down. My back immediately began complaining. I nodded at the smoking goombah. "Can I have one of those?"

He shook a cigarette loose from the pack and held it out for me. I took it from him and leaned forward while he flicked his lighter for me. Drawing at the cigarette heavily, I shut my eyes and held in the smoke.

"You fellows got any whiskey?" I asked.

Losurdo laughed. "Grandpa's having a party. Tommy, get him a drink."

If I was going to have to find a way to kill these bastards, I wasn't going to do it without a couple of belts on board.

28

CROSSED the yard in front of the cabin, standing for a moment on the edge of the trees looking around for Clint. There was no sign of him, but as soon as I stepped into the woods, I could see him squatting alongside a tree trunk. He stood as I came to him.

"I could have taken out those guys," he said, "but I didn't know if that was what you wanted."

"There's been enough shooting," I said. "I want to settle this without it."

We made our way back through the trees, across my lot, and back to the truck as I told Clint what had gone on in the cabin.

"Man," he said, "this is too much."

"I need to meet them again tomorrow," I said. "I don't know if they'll hold up their end or just try to shoot us all."

Clint walked a ways in silence, picking his way toward

the road. Finally, he said, "So what do these Cubans have to do with any of this?"

"Middlemen, I guess. They're talking like they're going to get a finder's fee or something."

We got to the truck and he drove us back to his cabin. When we'd gone a few miles, he spoke again. "Don't think you can trust anyone in this."

"Myself. You. Hartley. . . . That about covers it."

HE rolled up the dirt track to his house, taking the switchbacks quickly in the dark. Up in the clearing, he pulled to a stop. We climbed out. I started to speak, but Clint held up his hand to silence me. He bent down to the ground.

"Someone has been here," he said quietly.

I crouched down beside him. He pointed to a footprint barely visible in the dirt.

"A running shoe," he said. "None of us is wearing anything like that." He scanned the yard. Lights were on in the cabin but it was quiet.

"You go inside, " he said. "I'm gonna circle the property and see what there is to see."

"What if they're inside?" I asked, my mouth dry and my heart pounding again. I had been counting on a few hours of time to decompress and the thought of another run-in with someone was almost more than I could take.

"I'll be circling to come in the back," he said. "Just hold what you got 'til I get there."

"Okay. Sure," I said. I stood, but my knees quivered.

Clint ducked into the woods, moving in a low crouch. In a moment he had disappeared silently into the trees. I picked up my rifle from the truck and crept toward the cabin, feeling a precipitous sinking in my stomach.

My feet creaked on the boards of the porch. I opened

the door. Latoya sat at the table. She'd been watching the front door and stared at me, her eyes large.

"This'll teach you to leave me here by myself," she said, looking off to my left.

A figure flew out from behind the door and barreled into me. I fell to the floor and he was on top of me. The air came out of me in a single grunt. A gun was buried in my neck and a voice in my ear.

"We meet again, Ingram," he said. It was Benny, his breath hot and sour in my face. "I should kill you right now," he whispered.

He kicked me away and kept the pistol pointed at me. He looked like hell—his head still wrapped with a now dirty and bloody bandage, his clothes filthy, sunglasses astride his nose crookedly, one of the legs broken off.

"Drop the rifle or I really will shoot you," he said.

I looked from him to Latoya.

"I didn't invite him here," she said.

I put down the rifle and pushed it to the side.

"That's better, cowboy," he said. He stood unsteadily and pulled out a chair from the kitchen table. Keeping the gun on me, he picked up my rifle, sat, and took a deep breath.

"How did you find me here?" I asked, playing for time and curious at the same time.

He smiled. "Elementary, Watson," he said. "I dressed down as one of you good-old-boys and trolled that armpit of a bar you took me to. Today someone said they'd seen you pass through with that redneck who tried to kill me for insulting Hank, Jr. All it took was a trip to the county records office to find the deed to the McConneyhead homestead, then a stop at the fish-and-game store for a USGS map to show me where it was."

I stood, then sat at the table with him.

"Where's the notebook?" Benny asked.

"It's not here," I lied.

"Where's your friend, McConneyhead?" he asked, standing and walking to check the back door.

He poked the back door open and looked out into the dark, then pulled it to and locked it.

"Lock the front door, 'Toya," he said. She moved to the door and turned the dead bolt.

I stared at her. She looked back at me.

"What?" she asked defensively. "What do you want me to do? He's the one with the gun."

Benny smiled as he turned off the lights and sat back at the table. He pinched her cheek as she sat down. "She knows what side her bread is buttered on," he said, then turned back to me. "Now, where's the fucking notebook?"

"I don't have it," I said.

We sat in the dark. He leaned forward, the pistol in his hand lying on the table. "Bullshit," he said. "Now, I want that book or I'm gonna start taking you apart one limb at a time."

"I gave it back to the mob," I lied.

He stood up and aimed the pistol at me. "Listen, I hate this," he said, clearly enjoying it. "I'm just trying to do my job. Don't make me hurt you."

At that moment, something crashed through the front window. Benny turned to it as it thudded in front of us. A rock skipped across the floor.

Benny followed its course with his eyes. The front door crashed open in the same instant, the lock splintering. Clint flew through the door, did a shoulder roll off the floor, and landed with his rifle brought to bear. "Don't do it!" he shouted.

Benny brought the pistol toward him, but Latoya reached out and knocked Benny's arm away. Clint didn't hesitate. The rifle spat fire across the room. Benny fell backward, his leg exploding in a cloud of red.

"Fuck!" Benny said as he hit the floor.

Gunsmoke filled the room. Clint stood and took a couple of steps toward him, holding the rifle at the ready.

Benny writhed on the floor, both hands holding his leg. Clint kicked the pistol away. He handed me the rifle then bent over Benny.

"Who the hell are you?" Clint asked as he reached and undid Benny's belt and pulled it from his pants.

"You don't want to know," Benny said.

Cling wrapped Benny's leg with his belt and cinched it down. Benny gasped as the belt tightened down above his wound. Clint ripped open the pant leg and inspected the damage.

"Flesh wound," he said. "Tough guy. Didn't take much to knock you on your ass."

"Fuck you," Benny said, gritting his teeth.

"Tough guy," Clint said again, then he stood and put his foot onto Benny's leg wound.

Benny cried aloud and tried to pull away.

Clint pressed harder. "Now why don't you tell me who you are."

Benny cried again. "Fuck!" He pulled away and scooted across the floor. "You're fucking crazy," he said.

"Damn right," Clint said. "One hundred percent service-connected Post-Traumatic Stress Disorder with Anxiety Neurosis. Now I want to know who you are." He took another step toward Benny.

Benny scooted farther away. "Man! Okay! Shit, enough already!"

Clint took the rifle back from me, pulled up a chair, and sat over Benny. "I'm listening," he said.

For the first time since I'd known him, he seemed completely himself, his eyes alight, his movements powerful but relaxed.

Benny scooted up to sit against the wall of the cabin. He

sighed. "Man, this day has sucked." He took in the room with a glance, realized he had no other options, and began to speak. "Ingram here really stepped in it last year. He probably told you about the money that he took. Maybe he told you about the Swiss accounts. Some people contracted with me to see what I could find out about the money. They'd learned about Ingram and Latoya. She moved back to L.A. and started living awfully well for a woman who didn't work. So I got close to her to see what she knew."

"Got me strung out," she said and spat on the floor.

"Collateral damage," he said.

"Who sent you?" I asked.

"That's confidential," he said.

"Not the Cubans?"

He shook his head.

"Not the mob."

"Worse than either of them," he said.

"This is too hot," I said. "We gotta unload this." The mob, the FBI, the Cubans, and God-knows-who-else—that we all weren't already dead had to be considered something like a miracle. I'd been sitting on this hot potato for too long.

"Fucking A," Clint said.

"Listen," Benny said, "you're crazy if you give this shit to those mobsters or those loser Cubans. Either one of them will kill you once they get their hands on it."

Clint spat at the floor near Benny. "Bullshit," he said. "I'd sooner trust the mob."

Benny shook his head. "Suit yourselves, man."

Clint bent over him and inspected the leg wound. He loosened the tourniquet and scrutinized the leg some more. "Bleeding's about quit," he said. Pointing toward the bathroom, he said, "Bring me that first aid kit."

I went into the bathroom and looked about until I laid eyes on a plastic case sitting on a shelf. Inside were packs of four-by-fours, rolls of silk tape, a bandage scissors, and the like. I carried it out to Clint. Quickly, he removed the tourniquet and applied a bulky pressure dressing. Benny grimaced but acquiesced.

"You'll be fine," Clint said to Benny. He fished out some handcuffs we'd taken from the sheriff's car and dragged Benny across the floor to a pipe that ran down one wall.

"Man," Benny said, "chill the fuck out."

Clint cuffed him to the pipe. "He should keep," he said to me. "Now let's go get rid of this stuff and get your friend back."

29

Hartley

THE wise guys were a couple of drinks down the road and beginning to get sloppy. They had the TV on, watching reruns of *Kojak*. Losurdo had gone to lie down in the bedroom.

"Who loves ya, baby?" one of them said as Telly showed up rolling his lollipop around in his mouth.

"Greek prick," the other one said, "thinks he's such a fuckin' hardass."

They went on in this idiom for quite some time. My back was beginning to eat at me again. I made a great show of pulling the morphine out of my pocket. I unscrewed the top, shook out some pills, and washed down a couple of them with the whiskey.

"Hey, what'cha got there, Gramps?" the first one asked.

"Medicine," I said.

He snatched the pill bottle from my hand.

"Fuck me!" he said, looking at the bottle. "Grampa's getting high."

"I've got prostate cancer," I said. "It's eating its way through my spine."

"Hey, that's too bad," he said indifferently. He shook the pill bottle and unscrewed the top.

"Goddamn," he said, "you got a pharmacy in there."

"They're not very strong," I said. "Takes two or three just to take the edge off."

He poured several pills into his hand. "We got a long night to kill," he said as he tossed back several of the pills then threw the bottle to his buddy. The second greaseball poured out some pills and swallowed them.

"How about another round?" I asked.

The first one filled our glasses. I tilted my glass at them. "Cheers," I said.

They turned their glasses bottoms up and drained them. I took a sip of mine and stared at them.

"You're okay, Gramps," the first one said.

"Yeah," I said, "a laugh a minute." I figured it would take a half hour for the morphine to hit on top of the whiskey and they'd be snoring if they didn't stop breathing altogether.

It took most of the rest of the *Kojak* episode before they were both passed out. I stirred around to see if that would wake them, but they were deep in sleep. Their guns sat in shoulder holsters inside their coats, but I didn't want to risk it for the moment.

I looked about the trailer, then walked quietly into the kitchen. After pulling open a couple of drawers, I found a boning knife—a brown carbon steel blade with a worn wooden handle. I eyed the edge of the blade and ran it across a fingernail. Still pretty sharp and nice and thin with a wicked tapered point. Yes, this would do—easy to slip between some ribs and twist until it broke. I slid the blade up my sleeve, holding the handle backhanded and concealed.

I crept back out of the kitchen and along one wall to the back bedroom where Losurdo slept. He was the one I wanted. I heard the sound of coughing—deep, congested, musical coughs. I peered into the bedroom.

He sat on the edge of the bed, bent over, rocking as he coughed, blood on his lips. He wiped it away with a handkerchief. He worked at it, coughs within coughs, rumbles and gurgles and plosives. This went on literally for minutes. Finally, he began tapering off, drawing deep breaths and wiping at his mouth. The handkerchief was now almost totally red.

"Goddamnit," he wheezed. He rocked back and forth on the bed and blew his nose. "Oh, jeez."

He sat with his back to me. I could have killed him right then and there. He was a dead man already, though. I could see it—lung cancer. Killing him would be a gift. Better he stayed alive as long as possible to suffer through it. Just then, he turned and saw me standing in the doorway.

"Hey, Gramps," he said, "What'cha doin'? My boys giving you the run of the place?"

"They're sleeping," I said.

"They're no damn good." He stood, tossing the handkerchief away. "I got this lousy cough," he said.

"You're coughing up blood," I said.

He looked down. "Yeah. Fuck. The doctors says I got cancer and they can't do nothing about it. They want to give me chemotherapy and radiation. Fuckin' high-priced poison."

"We've all got something eating at us," I said. "Got different names, but it eats at us just the same."

"You got that right," he said. He looked at me. "You're okay, Gramps."

I stood back from the door as he walked into the living

room. As he walked past me, I carefully slipped the knife into my right front pocket and untucked my shirt to hide the handle. He looked disgustedly at his two men asleep on the sofa.

"They got into my pain pills," I said.

"You can't get good help these days," he said.

At that moment, the sound of a fist pounding on the front door drummed through the room. The trailer shook and rattled. The two men on the sofa didn't stir, but Losurdo produced a pistol from inside his jacket. He moved to the door, his back to the wall beside it.

"It's Mendoza!" a voice called from outside.

Losurdo peered out the window beside the door. He looked at me. "Open the door," he said.

I walked over to the door, turned the dead bolt, and opened it. Mendoza and one of his men stood on the steps.

"There's been a change in plans," Mendoza said. "We have to move now."

"What the fuck," Losurdo said. "Cops?"

"Ingram insists on meeting tonight to turn over the material," Mendoza said. "He said that it was urgent."

"Shit," Losurdo said. He began nudging then kicking on the sleeping greaseballs. "Jesus! Wake the fuck up."

They stirred and batted away Losurdo's prodding. He went to the kitchen and filled a pitcher and doused them both. They blinked and shook their heads and stared about blearily.

"Get the fuck up!" he said.

The two of them stood slowly, tucking in shirts, straightening collars, and checking their pieces, weaving a little bit on their feet.

"Get Grandpa," Losurdo said. "We gotta roll."

They nodded and one of them moved toward me, grabbing me by the arm and trundling me out the door.

30

Ingram

CLINT parked the truck about a quarter mile down the road from Buendia's cabin, this time on the side away from my cabin.

"Never establish a pattern," he said as he rolled to a stop along the road.

Latoya sat between us. She had refused to stay behind with Benny in the cabin, and I had been uncertain enough of her loyalties to leave her there. Clint and I climbed out and stood again by the side of the road, rifles in hand. With the door still open, I leaned into the cab of the truck.

"You can stay here and wait," I said to Latoya. "If you decide to take off, that's your business. Town's that way." I pointed.

"Where have I got to go?" she asked.

Clint and I set off into the trees. Living with this insanity had become so familiar by now that I didn't even pause to reflect on the absurdity of traipsing through the woods in the dead of night bearing automatic weapons and secret bank account numbers toward a rendezvous with the Mafia and middle-aged Cuban freedom fighters, stalked by anonymous powers and principalities. I was tired and unwashed and wrung out, finding myself contemplating my own possible demise with only an abstract concern for the inconvenience it might cause others. Surely Uncle Rayburn would curse me again when he was stuck with the funeral expenses of yet another feckless Ingram.

We made straight from the road down to the banks of the river, picking our way slowly through the trees. The night was cool and dry. The woods rustled and croaked and ruminated. Clint led the way surely. Following him, I wondered again just why he was doing all this. He'd refused to stay behind at the cabin and let me go alone.

"It's okay," he'd said. "I'll just lay back in the woods like last time."

"I don't want to get anyone else hurt," I'd replied.

He only looked at his feet and said, "It's okay. I want to do this. I'm breathing again for the first time in a long while."

His hands had shaken when he'd lit a joint and taken a couple of tokes off it on the way there. He'd punched up a country station on the car radio and driven in silence.

"I read those files on the computer," he'd said at last. "Some crazy shit."

Now walking behind him, I guess I understood why he was here—all the dread aside, the world had edge and meaning when informed by the possibility of sudden death and the necessity for violence. That was why men secretly yearned for war as a deliverance from the banality and malaise of everyday life and as a way into these states of clarity and keening adrenaline.

We came to the banks of the river and stood for a moment. Upriver and off to our right, we could see the lights of Buendia's cabin. The waters of the Sour Mash murmured past us, dark and rippling in the moonlight.

"We'll be less likely to be flanked coming up from the water," Clint said.

I nodded, winded a little from the walk in. We turned and picked our way upriver, a few yards in from the bank, Clint still leading, picking his way carefully among the tree roots and rocks and gullies. After about fifteen minutes, we stood on the bank in front of the cabin, which sat a good thirty yards up slope. We could see the house through the trees. A car and a pickup sat in the yard, but the Lincoln that the mobsters had driven was nowhere to be seen. I squatted beside a tree and laid my rifle up against it.

"We'll wait here until everyone shows up," I said. "I don't want to be surprised like I was last time."

Clint looked around.

"Let me reconnoiter the perimeter," he said. He set off farther upriver along the bank, the rifle held at the ready. In a moment I was unable to make him out among the trees.

A thin breeze blew through the trees. I shivered and my stomach rumbled. Man, this was getting old.

After about an hour, two pairs of headlights bumped down the road and into the clearing in front of the cabin. The first car looked like the Towncar and the second a nondescript sedan lost in the glare from the first. They rolled to a stop and the engines and lights died. Four men climbed out of the first car and two from the second. After milling about for a moment in the yard, they trooped up the stairs. One man remained out on the porch while the rest went inside.

I squatted in the dark and waited, picking up my rifle and flicking off the safety. After a few minutes, Clint appeared noiselessly off to my right, sifting from between the trees like the fog that was beginning to rise up off the river. He sat down next to me.

"One on the porch, five went inside," he said. "No one on the perimeter."

"Probably a few more who were already in there," I said.

"Not good odds."

"Yeah."

"So, you're going in?" he asked.

"I guess," I said.

"Let's do it this way," he said. "We'll take down this guy on the porch, then you negotiate this from the door while I take your back."

"Let's try hard not to shoot anyone," I said.

"Sure," Clint nodded. "Let me circle around and I'll come up beside the house. Then you walk up to the front steps, get his attention, and I'll take him down."

I nodded in the dark, my mouth dry, my heart pounding.

"Let's go," I said.

31

Hartley

WE sat again in the colonel's cabin—the same motley collection of over-the-hill Cubans and fish-out-of-water mobsters. I'd been playing up my debility in front of them all in order to get them to disregard me as a threat, but at this point I felt every ounce the tired, dirty, cancerous old man. But this made me twice as dangerous—low and mean and drugged-up on morphine with nothing to lose. I regretted not slicing that goombah's throat when I had the chance and for the moment couldn't decide if I'd passed because the thought of him dying slowly of lung cancer was more wicked, or if I'd simply lost my nerve.

"So, what the fuck is going on?" Losurdo asked, coughing thickly again.

"Ingram wants to get this over with," Mendoza said. "He sounded nervous on the phone."

"Well, were the fuck is he?" Losurdo asked.

"He said he'd be here," Buendia said.

Just then something thudded and crashed out on the front porch. The one greaseball inside and the Cubans reached for their guns. The door flew open, swung around, and crashed into the wall beside it.

"Tommy!" Losurdo yelled. "What's going on out there?"

Ingram peeked around the corner of the door, squatting low. "Tommy's busy," he said.

He glanced down toward the floor of the porch. "Tell 'em you're okay, Tommy," he said.

"Fuck," Tommy presumably said.

"He's all tied up right now," Ingram said. "I hope you'll excuse him." He reached down and produced a spool of duct tape and rolled it into the room.

"What the fuck do you want?" Losurdo asked. "It's fuckin' four in the morning."

"I want my friend back," Ingram said, standing but still shielding himself behind the wall of the cabin. Not that the wall would have done him much good — if anyone decided to shoot, the rounds would have gone right through the thin boards of this shack.

"What's the hurry all of a sudden?" Losurdo asked.

"Things are getting way too dangerous. I have the mob and Cubans and the FBI breathing down by neck, and now God-knows-who-else," he said. "I need to get rid of this shit before the KGB gets into the act."

The Cubans exchanged glances. The mobsters shifted around on their feet.

"So what d'ya got?" Losurdo asked.

Ingram stood full in the doorway, seeming to gain confidence. "I've got the encryption key here," he said, holding up an envelope. "Now, I want you to let Dr. Hartley go and leave us both alone in the future. He's going to come with me and we're going to leave the envelope on the front steps. If we don't get out of here safely, the FBI's gonna get a call and the originals."

Losurdo nodded to his lieutenant. He pulled me to my feet. "Go on, Grampa," he said.

I stood reluctantly, fingering the knife handle in my pocket. It looked like my opportunity for revenge was slipping away. Losurdo was perhaps three steps away from me. I could close the gap in an instant, take him from behind, and slit his throat. Would that be satisfactory? If I was lucky, they'd shoot me in the process, solving my other problems as well.

Just then the McConneyhead fellow appeared in the door beside Ingram. "Someone's coming through woods," he said to Ingram. "Two or three people from two directions."

Everyone turned to look at him. I seized the moment and came up behind Losurdo, wrapping my left arm around his neck and bringing the knife up to his throat.

"Don't move," I said, pressing the knife into his neck. We were close as lovers, my face up against his ear, his hair, his neck. I was breathing in the reek of his pomade, his cologne, his sweaty day-old funk. I whispered in his ear, "I can't decide whether to let the lung cancer eat you slowly or whether to kill you right now."

"Do it, old man," he said, holding up one hand to stay his henchman, who had turned toward us and brought his gun to bear.

I brought the knife up harder against his throat. The point pressed into the skin. A trickle of blood began to run down his neck. One more shove and I'd have been into his jugular vein. Another half-inch. I breathed deep. Shit. I relaxed my grip by the slightest degree.

That was all he needed. He brought his right elbow back into my ribs and his heel down hard on my foot. All the air left my lungs. My back buckled under the blow. I went down hard, falling and hitting the floor. An explosion of pain in my back with a sickening snap and crunch deep inside sent an electric shock down both my legs. I choked back a cry. The knife fell from my grip.

Losurdo stood over me, picking up the knife. "You should have done it while you had the chance. You'd'a done me a favor."

I tried to push myself back from him, but my legs wouldn't work. Rising up on my elbows, I crawled back against the wall, my legs trailing after me like dead weights.

The Cubans had their guns on Losurdo. In the moment's confusion, they had disarmed his henchman.

"Put down the knife," Mendoza said.

Losurdo looked up at them. "This old fuck tried to kill me," he said.

The pain in my back was searing. I gasped and pulled at the air.

Losurdo threw the knife across the room and stood up. "Okay," he said, "let's put away the fucking guns and finish our business here."

Ingram and McConneyhead now stood inside the cabin, peering out through the open door. Footfalls resounded on the front steps and porch.

"Hold it!" McConneyhead called out the door.

"It's all right," Buendia said, "they're with me." He knelt down beside me, motioning for me to be still for now.

Ingram turned to look at him. "What's going on here?" he asked.

Mendoza stepped forward. "We're going to take this off of Mr. Losurdo's hands."

"The hell you are," Losurdo said.

"You're finished," Mendoza said, suddenly vehement. "You're nothing without old man Trafficante. You think

we haven't been waiting for this? Thirty years he was
Fidel's bitch, whoring for him and we were watching.
Thirty years I watched him playing both ends against the
middle, selling cocaine for the Colombians, running
money and spying for Fidel, selling guns to us and disin-
formation to the CIA and FBI. And now it is our time."

"Don't fuck with me," Losurdo said.

Mendoza laughed. "You are no Trafficante. You're finished. Tampa's finished. You're all going to jail or to the
bottom of the sea."

Mendoza nodded to his men, who still had their guns at
the ready. The three men who had come up on the porch
from the dark now came inside the cabin as well. Mc-
Conneyhead and Ingram raised their rifles and let them
pass. Suddenly Losurdo and his man found themselves
surrounded by five armed Latinos.

Mendoza said something to the men in Spanish.

Losurdo flushed a lobster red. "Goddamnit!" he bellowed. "I can't believe you Spick bastards!"

"Believe it," Mendoza said. He caught the eye of one of
his men and made a slashing motion across his throat. The
man nodded.

They grabbed Losurdo and his man. The henchman
went quietly, pale as a fish belly, but Losurdo thundered
and fought. "Fuck you all!" he cried. "I'll fucking kill you
all!"

One of the Cubans cracked him across the face and they
hustled them both outside. They clattered down the steps
and out into the yard. Losurdo continued to bluster and
shout but in another moment there was the dull thud of
several blows and he fell quiet. The report of a pistol came
next. Two rounds, then a pause followed by two more
rounds, then another two. Then came silence.

"Jesus," Ingram said, looking out the door.

"I'm sorry for the disruption," Mendoza said. "But as

you can see, we've solved your problem with the Mafia and now we'd like to relieve you of the accounts and the encryption key."

"What just went on here?" Ingram asked.

I had found the morphine bottle and twisted off the top, downing four or five pills all at once. Buendia still knelt beside me, but his attention was on Mendoza and Ingram.

"We used you to lure these gentlemen down here," Mendoza went on. "Far away from their support where we could finish them. Others from our group are dealing with their compatriots back in Tampa."

"What is this? A gang war?" Ingram asked. "I thought you were freedom fighters."

"We must use whatever weapons that come within our reach. The Trafficante family was unraveling. It was time for us to use this moment to seize what we could of their operations . . . as a source of funding for our efforts."

"I see,'" Ingram said.

"Fidel has done as much for years with his trafficking of cocaine," Mendoza said. "We are only fighting fire with fire."

"Last time I checked, that didn't work too well," Ingram said. "Now just why is it that I'm going to turn over everything to you?"

"As I said," Mendoza went on, "we have solved your problem for you. And as you've said, you want to be rid of the burden of the information you have. So, we would be happy to oblige and take it off your hands."

"You're gonna kill us, too," Ingram said.

"No," Buendia said, standing, "I have guaranteed your safety and continue to do so." He turned to one of the Cubans. "Luis," he said, "give me your gun."

Luis looked at Buendia, surprised at the request. He glanced at Mendoza, who nodded his head. Luis turned the machine pistol over to Buendia.

Now Buendia turned to the other Cuban. "And now, you, Miguel, give me your pistol."

Miguel turned over his gun. Buendia stood holding both the guns. "Now you see," he said to Ingram, "we do not threaten you. You want to be rid of this thing. Your friend is injured." He inclined his head toward me. "Let's end this."

Ingram looked over at McConneyhead then down at me. The three Cubans who had been outside came up the steps and inside the cabin. They were younger and harder-looking fellows than the two with Mendoza, dressed in camos with bootblack under their eyes. The lead man looked at Buendia and nodded.

Buendia turned back to Ingram. "The envelope," he said.

32

Ingram

THREE men had just been executed in the front yard, and the room was full of men with guns. Hartley lay huddled against the wall, the smell of cordite mixing with the sweaty odor of fear that still hung in my nostrils after they had hustled two mobsters past me to be shot in the yard. I'd seen their eyes—Losurdo wild and raging, the younger one's eyes blank and withdrawn. They'd clubbed Losurdo to his knees, though he cursed and fought the whole way, and finished him with a couple of shots to the back of the head. He slumped into the leaves, suddenly still like a sack of feed. The younger one settled meekly to his knees with one push. He turned to look back over his shoulder as one of the Cubans finished him with another two shots to the back of the head. Then they pulled the third one off the front porch. They slung him onto the ground and delivered another two shots.

These Cubans were young, lethal-looking fellows with

dead eyes. They held MAC-10s lightly at their hips and stood near the doorway.

And now this guy wanted me to hand over the envelope. I'd had enough. Three more were dead and Hartley was hurt and it suddenly didn't matter anymore. I reached into my pocket.

"We have your guarantee of safety?" I asked.

He nodded.

I looked at Hartley then at Clint. Hartley had a faraway, glazed look, in obvious pain. Clint stood with his back to the wall, his eyes darting. He had worked his way behind the field of vision of the young Cubans and seemed coiled tight and ready to spring. I needed to get help for Hartley and to keep Clint from taking matters into his own hands and maybe getting himself killed. I handed over the envelope.

Buendia stepped forward and took in from me, meeting my eyes firmly and nodding.

"You have done the right thing," he said. He then raised his eyes to the young Cubans and said something in Spanish.

I stepped away from them, putting my back to the wall as I saw Clint do the same. We swung our guns toward them, but the three just walked past us and encircled Mendoza and his two men.

"What is this?" Mendoza asked, bewildered at the weapons suddenly turned on him. Buendia still held the weapons he'd taken from Mendoza's two lieutenants.

Buendia said the same Spanish phrase to the men.

It was Mendoza's turn to pull away against the wall. He asked something in Spanish.

"Did you think I did this for you?" Buendia asked, talking now in English perhaps for our benefit, perhaps so the *pistoleros* couldn't understand.

Mendoza looked genuinely confused.

"I am taking the money," Buendia said.

"For yourself?" Mendoza asked.

"For Cuba," Buendia said. "You think you represent Cuba, but you're no better than the criminals you want to replace in Tampa. *Freedom fighters!*" He spat. "I was with Fidel in the mountains. We were freedom fighters. Revolutionaries. You are nothing more than *degenerado*."

"What?"

Buendia nodded. "I've seen the things you have done, the beds you've slept in, the bodies you have buried, trying to replace the *Revolucion* with more of your Batista mobster corruption. And now you want to replace the Trafficantes in Tampa and then bring it back to Cuba?"

"And what will you do with the money?" Mendoza asked.

"Keep it away from you," he said. "Take it back to Cuba when the time is right. It will be useful after Fidel has passed."

Mendoza turned his head and spat at Buendia's feet. "You are the *degenerado*," he said. "You are taking this money to put away for your old age. And you are going to kill us to conceal your treachery."

Buendia shook his head. "Do not be afraid. I will send you on your way and let you continue to dream your old man dreams." He nodded to his men and they shepherded Mendoza and his two lieutenants toward the door.

"We will track you down," Mendoza said as he left. "You will not spend another night in peaceful sleep."

Buendia nodded. "I have not known a peaceful night's sleep in forty years. Why should I start now?"

When they were gone, he turned back to me. "There is something else you have," he said. "It is even more dangerous to you than this notebook."

I did not reply, waiting to hear what else he knew. Clint was kneeling at Hartley's side.

"Papers or files," Buendia said. "Memoirs of the man you killed last year. The mobster."

I still held my tongue, not wanting to tip my hand.

"We do not have much time," he said. "These files, if you have them, will only cause you harm."

"Why?" I asked.

He drew close to me. "You don't want to know."

"Try me," I said.

"Have you looked at the files?" he asked.

I nodded. "Briefly."

"This man was Trafficante's right hand for a number of years. Trafficante was Castro's principal contact in the American mob."

I nodded. "So I've been told."

"There are certain matters they pursued together. Matters that more than a few people would like to see never reach the light of day."

Clint got up from Hartley's side. "This guy's a spinal case," he said. He grabbed the front door and pried and pulled the pins in the hinges. The door came loose and he carted it to Hartley. He pushed away the kitchen table and laid the door flat alongside Hartley.

"We gotta get him into the hospital," he said.

We both turned and crossed the room. Hartley lay slumped against the wall. Clint pulled him down flat onto the floor.

I knelt beside him. He had a glassy look to his eyes. "Are you okay?" I asked.

"Screwed up something in my back," he said between gritted teeth. "I can't move my legs."

"He's got a spinal injury," Clint said. "Help me log-roll him onto the door."

We rolled him onto the door, Hartley grimacing and cursing under his breath. He came to rest lying on his back again, gasping in pain.

"That your pickup out there?" Clint asked Buendia.

Buendia nodded.

"Back it up to the porch and we'll load him into the bed of the truck."

"We'll talk later," Buendia said to me, rising and heading out the front door.

33

Hartley

THEY rolled me around like a bag of manure, then hoisted me up on that old door and set me on the kitchen table. McConneyhead grabbed the roll of duct tape and ran some around the door to tape down my hips, feet, and shoulders. He worked quickly, nervously, snugging me down to the door until I felt as dressed out and trussed up as a Thanksgiving turkey. This is what it had come to.

"You a medic in the service?" I asked, trying to take my mind off the pain.

"No, sir," he said. "But I packaged a few folks for transport in my time."

In a few moments I was strapped down. He and Ingram then picked me up off the table and headed toward the door. They had to tilt the door somewhat to get me through the doorway, but the tape held me down pretty good. It was a shame. This McConneyhead kid was putting up such a good fight to get me into the hospital when I was pretty

sure it was all useless, my cancerous spine having col-
lapsed and crushed the nerve roots in my back past the
point of being salvaged. I was done.

The morphine had begun to take hold and the pain
faded as they trundled me into the bed of the truck. In the
glow of the morphine, my fate began to take on an abstract
and academic air, as if I were considering the state of a
specimen laid out on my dissecting table. McConneyhead
and Ingram settled into the bed beside me, squatting low
and hanging on to the sidewalls.

"Why don't you ride up front," Clint said to Ingram.
"I'll sit here with him."

"No, that's okay," Ingram said. "I'll sit with him. You
sit up front and keep that guy honest."

Clint nodded and climbed out of the bed and into the
cab. The engine thrummed and we began bouncing down
the rutted road toward the highway. Each bump and jolt
sent deep, visceral pain through my back and electrical
stabbing down my legs.

"You okay?" Nelson asked, bending over me. He took
off his coat and draped it over me.

I had had that son-of-a-bitch by the throat and the knife
to his jugular, my nostrils full of his days-old red meat
reek, tobacco and sweat and booze. I had William's death
on my back, his revenge to take, and I couldn't do it. I'd
hesitated, flinched—an old man losing his nerve at the
crucial moment. In the next moment I was on the floor in
pieces, a broken old man.

"I'm okay," I said to Ingram quietly.

"We're gonna get you to the hospital," he said.

The truck bounced heavily as we left the dirt road and
came onto the highway, and a cry of pain escaped my lips
before I could strangle it. Ingram fretted and pulled help-
lessly at the coat that covered me. Goddamnit, was this
what it all came to? Seventy-five years invested to come to

this? My son gone, my wife eaten up by cancer, my best friend murdered, denied even revenge, and now even my independence gone, paralyzed and lying in my own urine strapped to a door in the back of a pickup, being driven around by a redneck and a Cuban vigilante. Shit. I finally just had to laugh out loud, though it hurt like hell. God is a helluva comedian, even if often He's the only one who gets the joke. Perhaps I'd be seeing Him soon and could give Him a piece of my mind.

They stopped a moment later on the shoulder of the road. McConneyhead climbed out of the cab. "I'm gonna follow you in my truck," he said.

"I won't go to a nursing home," I said.

"What?" Ingram asked. The poor boy was confused. Not that I was any better off. What the hell had I been doing with myself for the last twenty years? What the hell was I doing now? Going to a goddamn hospital? For what?

"Cut this goddamn tape off of me," I said. I'd had enough of this.

"I don't think we should," Nelson said.

"Just cut the tape off me," I thundered at him.

He looked hesitantly around for direction. Finally he produced a pocketknife and cut through the duct tape that held me down to the board. I pushed it away, freeing my arms and then hips and legs. Things felt better already.

I pulled Ingram's coat off me, bunched it up, and stuffed it behind my head. Rising up on my elbows, I pushed myself back until my head and then my shoulders rested against the back wall of the pickup bed. Any movement caused great spasms of pain in my back and legs, but I kept pushing until I was almost sitting up. It hurt more than anything ever had, but finally I could see over the side-walls of the truck. Overhead the sky was full of stars, Orion climbing up the horizon from the east. The roaring pain in my back, the ruin of my body and life, the nullity

of all my plans and ambitions, and this goddamn beautiful
autumn night were of a piece. How could the world be so
fucking beautiful and yet have such a bottomless ability to
inflict pain and take from us all that we value?

Despite it all, because of it all, the world was never
more vivid, the air never sweeter to breathe, the woody autumnal smells never more redolent and evocative. It
seemed I could remember the last seventy-five autumns—
red-orange leaves and wood smoke and the slanting of
long westering light in the crisp, chill air. I remembered
family Thanksgivings, frigid mornings walking the fields
with a bird-dog, afternoons of football and bourbon and
storied, irrelevant loyalties and enmities. All gone. Pissed
away and lost and dead and gone. Goddamnit.

"I need a cigarette," I said. I'd wedged myself into the
corner of the pickup bed and it felt better.

"What?" Ingram asked again.

"A cigarette. I need a cigarette. And a drink."

"We need to get you to the hospital," he said in a pleading tone.

"My back's gone," I said. "My legs are gone. There's no
hurry. Just get me a cigarette and a bourbon."

The door of the truck popped open again, the dome
light from the cab spoiling my appreciation of the stars.

"Shut off that light!" I said, irritatedly. "I'm trying to
find the Pleiades."

The door snapped shut obediently. This was my
deathbed, shabby as it was, and I was damned if I was
going spoil things by being too polite.

"What's the matter?" Buendia asked.

"He wants a cigarette," Ingram said.

"And a shot of whiskey," I said.

The Copley woman appeared from I don't know where,
peering into the pickup bed. "Jesus," she said, "what are
you crazy crackers up to?"

"No good, honey," I said. "You should have stayed in L.A."

"You got that right," she said.

"Dr. Hartley," McConneyhead said, "you really should be lying down."

"Son," I said, turning to look at him, "I'm not some nineteen-year-old grunt with a gunshot wound and this isn't Vietnam. I'm a cancerous old fart with an eaten-up spine and no time left. Now, I appreciate your efforts and concern, but I'm not salvageable."

He backed away a step, looking hurt.

"No offense, McConneyhead," I said. "I know you mean well. But the war's been over for fifteen years now. Life's too goddamn short to be spending it hiding out in the woods spooked by things that're long gone. I ought to know.

"And you, Ingram. Drinking away your pirate's treasure in that sad little shack in the woods. You ought to be glad it burned down. Maybe it'll get your father's ghost off your back and let you get on with a life."

"There. I've said my piece. Now if you'll just give me a smoke and drink, I'll go quietly."

"Someone want to tell me what went on here?" the Copley woman asked.

"Later," Ingram said.

Buendia reached into his coat pocket and produced one of his cigars and a flask.

"Not what I was looking for, but it'll do," I said.

He handed it to me then flicked out a Zippo. I pulled at the cigar until it got going. Raucous, heady stuff. I drew it all the way in. Fucking marvelous. Next came the hip flask. I unscrewed the cap and pulled at it. Rum. Nipping at the flask and puffing on the cigar, I spent a graceful few minutes there in the dark of the roadside, staring up at the stars while the rest of them stood around, baffled but respectful. I was really looking forward to meeting God. I figured Him for a bastard of cosmic proportions, but perhaps a complex fellow capable of enjoying a good smoke and snort.

At last, I handed the cigar back to Buendia. "Thank you," I said.

He took the cigar and dropped it to the ground, snuffing it out, looking contemplatively at his feet, then back up at me.

"Let's go, boys," I said, keeping the flask.

Meekly, Buendia climbed back into the truck, while McConneyhead and the Copley woman walked back to his truck. Ingram sat beside me, quizzical and shivering in the cold. In a moment we were back on the road. I fished the morphine vial from my pocket and shook a half-dozen or more pills into my palm, tossed them into my mouth, then chased them with a healthy splash of rum. The fire in my belly and the fire in my back seemed to be the only alive parts of me. At last I scooted lower in the truck, resting my head again on Ingram's coat, starting to shiver myself now in the cold.

I sighed and looked up at the stars. I felt a sudden ache high in my chest and tears came to my eyes. I blinked them away and gritted my teeth. Shit. Everything hurt. Even the things that felt good hurt when you lost them. What was the point? Revenge hadn't even worked for me.

I'd sent my son, Andrew, off to war. He'd asked my advice. It was 1967 and the handwriting on the wall had been plain for some time. We all knew we were being lied to and that the cause was a bad one. If I'd have just said the word, he'd had gone off to Canada and safety, or at least to jail in honorable dissent. But instead I told him he was a man and needed to make up his own mind and he'd gone and enlisted. Thought I'd raised him better, but what could I say then? And within a year, the Army returned him in a bag, blown up somewhere in the Mekong Delta. The best of me left the world with him. And I didn't even have God to blame for that one. The foolishness and vanity of man took my son. I should have known better and I could have protected him.

My chest heaved as I fought off sobs, embarrassed but feeling myself spinning to pieces, unable to keep myself under control. What a mess it all was.

"You okay, Seymour?" Nelson asked.

"Shit, Nelson," I said, "I'm all in. I'm sorry."

"You're going to be okay," he said.

"Bullshit. I'm done. You need to get out of this town and get on with your life."

Nelson just sat there. "Yeah," he said finally.

I leaned forward and sipped at the flask. Mother Rum, I'll miss you. I washed down another handful of morphine with a healthy gulp.

Time to go.

34

Ingram

HARTLEY looked like hell huddled in a corner of the pickup bed. I couldn't get him to lie down flat. He just sat there, drinking out of the hip flask, grimacing and looking up at the sky, occasionally talking out of his head. I saw him swallow some pills and stash a vial away in his pocket.

The early morning was cold and still. We rocked back and forth as Buendia drove us into town. I thought again of that trip to Washington with my father. We'd left for home in the late afternoon after the Lincoln Memorial. He'd driven straight through, stopping only for gas and coffee. I'd sat beside him on the seat and afternoon faded into evening and then night and then early morning. He'd said little. I was hungry and tired. On a stretch of two-lane highway somewhere close to home the car drifted more and more toward the centerline. The headlights of the on-coming traffic were blinding. I felt the car speeding up and the trucks and cars seemed to thunder past us. A few began honking their horns. Still, my father kept his eyes straight ahead, staring into the headlights.

"Dad?" I said finally. "Are you okay?"

As if stirred from a dream, he turned to look at me and blinked, then looked back at the oncoming cars. His foot came off the gas and the car moved away from the center-line.

"I'm okay," he said, his voice deep and distant as if coming from the bottom of a well.

His chest heaved with a sigh. He turned to look at me again. "It's a difficult business," he said. "I don't know what to tell you. They're going to break your heart, and whatever you have, they'll take it away."

He shook his head. "I don't know what to tell you."

Soon afterward he was dead. I'd been sick ever since wondering what I could have done to change things. What could anyone have done?

As we came into town, Hartley looked over at me. "Fuck 'em if they can't take a joke," he said, sounding thick tongued and sleepy.

I nodded, not sure what he meant. He'd been talking like that ever since we'd pulled over and let him have the hip flask.

"Okay," I said.

"I'm not going to no nursing home," he said.

"Who'd said anything about a nursing home?" I said. "We're gonna get you taken care of."

"Just cremate me and scatter my ashes in Bryant Denny Stadium," he said.

"They have artificial turf there. You'd just get vacuumed up."

He lay back in the bed of the truck, watching the sky pass overhead. "Used to do this as a boy," he said. "Lie on my back in the backseat while my father drove and watch the trees and telephone poles and power lines go past. Trying to figure out where we were. I'd say we're coming into town right now."

"That's right."

"Where did it all go?" he asked.

"Where did what go?"

"Life. My whole goddamn life."

"It just goes."

We bumped up the driveway of the hospital and rolled toward the loading area in front of the ER.

"We're here," I said.

The bright pools of light and the gleaming windows and glass doors seemed like a welcoming little island of sanity in this long dark night. We came to a stop in front of the electric doors.

"No machines," Hartley said. "No codes, no tubes."

He looked down at his feet as Clint showed up with a trio of the ER crew. "If you let that butcher Bebe work on me, I sue your pants off," he said to them.

"It's Dr. Hartley," one of them said as he climbed into the truck bed. Another followed after him with an ER backboard. In a few moments they had rolled him onto the board and strapped him down, hoisted him over to a waiting stretcher, and wheeled him inside.

As they sped up the ramp, he raised his head and looked back at me as I stood watching from the truck. "Get on with your lives," he said. "All of you!" And then he was gone up the ramp and into the ER, Buendia walking with him.

Clint and Latoya stood at my side, having parked nearby.

"He's right, y'know," Clint said.

"What?"

"Life's too damn short to spend it hiding out spooked in the woods."

"He was drunk and high on pain pills. He didn't mean anything by that."

"No, he's right. Fuckin' war was over fifteen years ago." He shook his head and chewed his lip. "Fifteen years."

"What about the computer files?" I asked him.

He shrugged. "I don't know, man. It's, like, ancient history. I don't know why anybody cares about them."

Buendia walked back out of the ER. We all stood together for a moment beside his truck in the parking lot.

"I have to go soon," he said. "As soon as the word gets out that Hartley and you have turned up, the FBI will be all over this place. And I've got three bodies in my yard."

"I still don't see why I should give you these files," I said.

"As long as you hold them, you are in danger and people will continue to come after you."

"What's to stop them from coming after me anyway, even after I give them to you?"

He nodded. "The government will soon learn you do not have them. My people will have what they want."

"But why should I trust you to do anything? You just want to keep the material from seeing the light of day like everyone else."

He smiled ruefully. "Fidel is old. Soon he will be gone. You think I want those fat Batistas to get back in power? So we can go back to the days when mobsters and sugar companies ruled Havana?" He shook his head. "The money and these files will give me influence and many cards to play after Fidel is gone. I can use them to help my people and perhaps to see that a democratic leader makes his way into power."

I looked him in the eyes as we stood in the lights outside the ER. I'd been lied to so many times by so many people that the truth seemed a fugitive now, not to be trusted when glimpsed. His eyes were dark, but steady, framed with crow's-feet, the skin tanned and swart.

"You're dreaming," I said. "Or lying."

He laughed aloud. "The vanity and dreams of another old man? Perhaps. But time is short. Will you give them to me?"

"Just get rid of it," Latoya said. "Ain't nothing good come of it."

I looked at Clint. He looked from Buendia and back to me. "Fuck it," he said and pulled the floppy disks from his jacket pocket. I took them and handed them to Buendia.

He put them quickly into his pocket. "*Gracias*," he said. "And I have something for you in exchange." From a pocket he produced a set of keys on a chain. He handed them to me.

"On the chain there is a tag with an address written on it. These are the keys to a safe house in at Dauphin Island. If the need arises, you can go there and lay low for as long as you want."

"How do you know the house is safe?"

"Nobody knows about that house," he said. "Not your government, not my government."

"Do you think the need will arise? I thought this would be the end it."

"You never know."

I put the keys into my pocket.

"I must leave soon, but first I want to go inside and pay my respects to Dr. Hartley," he said.

We went inside and Buendia walked back to the treatment area with such an air of authority that the nurses just let him pass.

The light seemed blinding inside. It was after five in the morning and the waiting room was empty except for a little old black lady who sat in a corner of the room beside the Coke machine, in an overcoat with two tattered grocery bags at her feet. Latoya, Clint, and I took seats in the waiting room. I chose a chair in the corner, putting my feet on the two chairs beside it. Inside of a minute, I was asleep.

35

Ingram

DARK shapes descended around me, a sudden scuffling and hubbub filling the room. I opened my eyes.

I was still in the ER waiting room. Jack Edmonds stood over me with dark-suited junior G-men behind him. Clint and Latoya were nowhere to be seen. I looked at the clock on the wall. Only about ten minutes had passed since I had sat down.

Jack squatted down and looked me in the eyes.

"Nelson," he said, "where ya been, ol' buddy?" His face looked care-worn and puffy, a forced smile on his lips, but his eyes probing, his brow furrowed and tense.

"You've been working down here too long," I said, sitting up in my chair.

"You've been missing for two days," Jack said. "You were supposed to meet me at the police station with your . . . materials."

"Events conspired against me," I said.

Jack turned to the dark-suited types behind him. "Can you excuse us for a moment?" he asked.

Jack grabbed me by the arm and roughly helped me to my feet. "Then let's talk outside for a minute, Nelson."

We moved quickly to the door and were standing back outside on the curb alongside the ER. The first gray suggestions of dawn had started to assert themselves along the eastern sky, the air chilly, a thin breeze blowing past making me shiver. Buendia's and Clint's trucks were gone. We stood together staring out at the brightening horizon, our breath steaming in the cold air.

"You're in a world of shit, Nelson," he said calmly.

It seemed to have become the usual state for my affairs, so the news did not really faze me. "How so, Jack?"

"Events have been conspiring against you at my end of the street, too," he said. "What did you do with the notebook you had?"

I hesitated. "It's a long story," I said.

"I'll take the *Reader's Digest* version."

"They were taken from me."

"By whom?"

"I'm not sure. People with very large guns."

"Mobsters?"

"No. They tried, but that's another story. Cubans, I think. Anti-Castro Cubans. They killed the mobsters and took the notebook."

He turned to look me in the eyes again. "Don't bullshit me, Nelson."

"No shit," I said.

"Then why didn't they kill you too?" he asked.

"I don't know," I said. "One of them seemed to know Hartley. He fell and hurt his back. They helped me bring him to the ER, then they left. They took everything."

Edmonds drew close to me. "Do you know who's with me in the waiting room right now?"

I looked back toward the room. The two of them stood watching us through the window.

"Junior G-men?" I asked.

"And you used to be a reporter?" Jack said. "The one in the off-the-rack wool blend suit is mine. But the one wearing the Italian-cut silk is CIA. A spook. He's been crawling up my ass since you disappeared after that shootout at the bank. He wants that notebook and whatever else you have. Bad. Now, I don't want to go tell him that you were robbed by some Cuban vigilantes. I'm not quite sure what he'd do with that news."

"What do you want me to do?"

"Damnit, Nelson, we were friends for a while years ago and that'll only get you so far." He was getting pretty hot. "You've been fucking with me over this case for more than a year. You didn't come clean with me last year, so don't be fucking with me now. I need to know everything that you know."

I looked at him. Who was I supposed to trust?

"The notebook had Swiss bank account numbers," I said. "But they were encrypted. I found the encryption key in a separate set of documents that I also got from the warehouse last year. I have no idea what's in those accounts. But I only gave them photocopies. I still have the originals."

He brightened. "Where are the originals?"

"They're with a friend."

"Not that line again. Where are they?"

"A friend. I can take you to him."

"What were these other documents you mentioned?" he asked.

"Files. Stuff." I looked over at the men in the waiting room. They seemed to be watching us intently.

Jack grabbed me by the arm. "Don't fuck around, Nelson! What were they?"

"Text files on some floppy disks. The memoirs of one of the mobsters who got killed last year."

"Where are they?"

"Why are they so important?" I said, now feigning ignorance. "I thought everyone just wanted the money."

"Do you know what's in them?"

I shrugged. "I didn't have time to read any of them. Why do they care about some mobster's memoirs?"

Jack shook his head. "You don't want to know. Just tell me where the files are."

"I don't have them," I said. "The Cubans took them too."

"You didn't keep copies?"

"No. Not of them. At the time I didn't think they were valuable."

Just then, the spook came out of the waiting room and walked up to us. "We don't have all day, Edmonds," he said. "Does this guy know anything?"

Jack looked from me to him. "He has the account numbers but some Cubans got copies of them, so we have to move fast before they can access them."

"And the other?" he asked.

"He had those, too, but the Cubans got them."

The spook looked upset. He brought a stack of photos out of his coat pocket. "Cubans?" he asked me. "How old?"

"Late middle age. Anti-Castro refugees," I said.

He flipped through the photos and pulled out a few and showed them to me. "Any of these look familiar?"

He had Mendoza and Buendia there. I nodded, feeling like I was going down the slippery slope toward betrayal. "Those two," I said, pointing to them.

He held up Buendia's photo. "Do you know who this man is?" he asked.

I shook my head. "He said his name was Buendia."

"Yeah. Buendia. One of his aliases—it's the name of a character from some novel. He thinks it's funny. This is Carlos Alarcon. Was very big in the anti-Castro Cuban community, but he dropped out of sight about a year ago. We have recent information that indicates he's been one of Castro's agents in this country since the early sixties."

"What?"

"Castro's man inside the anti-Castro community. Where is he now?"

My mouth worked wordlessly, flapping like a guppy. "I don't know," I got out at last. I'd given up everything to a communist double agent.

The agent turned to Jack. "We have to move on this," he said. "This guy could be out of the country before we know it."

"We need to get that notebook," Jack said.

"Sure," I said, glancing around, wondering where Clint and Lotoya had gone.

36

Ingram

WE drove out of town and into the country as dawn
broke. I sat in the back bracketed by Edmonds and
the Italian suit while the off-the-rack agent drove. We
made our way into the country toward Clint's cabin. I had
no idea where he'd disappeared. On the way there I tried
to get them ready for what we were about to encounter, and
told them about Benny breaking in on us and getting shot,
and how we'd left him cuffed to a pipe. They all listened
politely but didn't respond.

After a half-hour we wound our way deeper into the
hills and approached Clint's property. They drove up the
narrow switchback up to Clint's cabin and rolled to a stop
in the clearing at the top of the trail. The cabin was quiet,
nothing stirring in the yard. Clint's pickup truck sat in the
yard, near the house. The sun had yet to clear the hills in
the hollow where the cabin lay, a gray light filling the
clearing, the surrounding woods dim.

"Is anyone here?" Edmonds asked.

The agents climbed out of the car and looked around the yard.

"Check out the house," Edmonds said to the other agent.

I climbed out. "Let me go inside first," I said, uncertain as to what I'd find. "The owner's a little jumpy."

Edmonds looked from me to the other agents, then back to me. "Okay," he said. He looked at the other FBI agent. "Go with him and wait on the porch." Then Jack turned to the spook. "Stay in the damn car. You're not supposed to be here in the first place."

The CIA agent scowled and held his ground beside the car.

I turned to walk toward the cabin, the other agent at my shoulder. Clint's pickup creaked and ticked, the engine cooling.

"Who lives here?" the agent asked.

"Friend of mine," I said. "A loner. A jumpy sort of guy, so let me go in first and make sure things are okay."

He nodded, scanning the yard and taking up a position at the base of the steps, while I climbed up to the door.

The front door was ajar, creaking open under my knuckles as I knocked. From my vantage the room was empty. I pushed the door the rest of the way open and stepped inside.

Benny sat against the wall, still cuffed to the pipe. He looked like hell, his head still festooned with the bloody bandage, his leg wrapped with the pressure dressing Clint had applied, the rest of his leg brown and crusted with dried blood.

He stared at me listlessly. I turned and called out the open door. "It's okay. Just the prisoner in here."

The sound of footsteps came creaking up toward the door. After a moment, the agent peered into the room, the muzzle of his pistol preceding him. He looked around the room then settled on Benny where he sat.

"John Smith?" the agent asked.

Benny nodded. "Ten-four," he said.

"It's okay, Ingram," the agent said, "he's with us." He stepped into the room and lowered his pistol.

"What?"

"Well, not with us," he equivocated. "He's with them," he said, nodding toward the yard.

"Them?" I asked.

"The Agency," Benny said.

"You're a fucking spook?" I asked, incredulous.

"Well, he's not really with them," the agent said. "You got the keys to those cuffs?"

"On the table," I said.

I wasn't following this. Just then, Edmonds came into the room.

"The Agency's barred by statute from pursuing operations within the U.S.," Edmonds said. "Mr. Smith here was working under an *arrangement* with them."

"What—like a bounty hunter? A subcontractor?"

"Did you get the goods from him?" Benny asked.

"The notebook's supposed to be here," Edmonds said.

"Arrest this asshole and let's get out of here."

"Arrest me?" I asked.

"You shot me and left me for dead handcuffed to a pipe," Benny said.

I started getting angry. "This man kidnapped me! He pistol-whipped me! He shot a sheriff's deputy! He broke into my friend's cabin and threatened us with a gun!"

"That's enough, Nelson," Edmonds said to me. "It wouldn't take much for me to bring you up on half-a-dozen federal charges, so you'd better keep your mouth shut."

"Jack!" I said. "I can't believe you're in on this shit! Do you know what these people are all about?"

Jack moved toward me and grabbed me. "Come with me," he said and pulled me out onto the porch. I staggered after him as he kept his grip on me. Out on the porch, he let go of me with a push.

"Don't preach to me, Ingram!" he said, his tall, powerful frame seeming to tower over me.

I stumbled but caught myself. "Jesus, Jack," I said, "you can't trust these people." I stood pressed against the rails of the porch. At the far end of the yard, the spook stood watching us curiously.

"You talk like you know me," he said, his nostrils flaring. He looked like he wanted to lay hands on me again. "Well, you don't know me. You don't know shit. You haven't seen the bodies I've buried. The world is a cold mother-fucking place and your goddamn Boy Scout ethics just don't work here. Maybe that's why you've been a damn drunk your whole life and why you're rotting in this godforsaken cracker backwater."

He took a deep breath and drew himself back to his full height.

"I don't have that luxury," he said after a pause. "I got kids to clothe and feed, and a job I can't afford to lose, and a chain of command to respect. Don't you think I like to arrest all these fancy-pants spooks? But I've got my orders. And your freedom's hanging by a thread. So don't goddamn push me."

We stood there for a moment. Jack adjusted his jacket and shot a cuff.

The spook walked across the yard toward us. Edmonds watched him approach.

"You think I like putting up with these people?" he asked.

"So, what do we got here?" the spook asked.

Benny appeared in the front door.

"Mr. Smith," the spook said, "we were wondering what had happened to you."

"We need to wrap this up," Benny said. "Haul this fucker in."

"Ingram's been cooperating with the investigation," Edmonds said.

"We need to bring him anyway," the spook said. "For safe keeping."

Edmonds looked at his fellow agent, then reluctantly reached for his handcuffs.

"Sorry, Nelson," he said. "We can sort this out later."

"Goddamnit, Jack." I took a step away from him and ended up backed against the rail of the porch.

The rail beside me exploded and splintered, followed close behind by the whistle and crack of a rifle shot. Everyone dropped, seeking cover behind whatever was handy, turning to the direction of the shot. I just stood there, two steps behind everyone else, still trying to figure out why I was being arrested.

Another shot spattered into the ground near the spook, sending him skittering for cover toward the car. I had made out the muzzle blast in the woods.

"Anybody hit?" Edmonds asked, hunkered down behind the rails of the porch.

No one answered.

In the silence a voice came from out in the woods. "Let him go!" It was Clint.

Benny had already ducked back inside the house. The second FBI agent was standing inside the house, peering out the doorway.

Another round thunked into the footings of the house and Clint shouted again, "Let him go!"

I stepped forward.

"Get the hell down, Nelson," Jack said.

"What? So you can arrest me?"

"We can work this out," he said.

"Sure," I said, "we'll do lunch."

I clambered down the steps and headed toward the trees. I looked around but couldn't spot Clint. I wasn't sure what I was going to do when I got clear of the cabin. The agents all squatted behind cover and watched me go.

I came to the trees and made my way into the woods. Ten yards in, the cover became thicker, the light dim, the leaves dripping with dew. I still couldn't see where Clint was, so I just continued to pick my way deeper into the woods.

Shots rang out from another direction, keeping the agents pinned down at the cabin. Up ahead I saw Clint set up behind a fallen tree still with his rifle trained on the cabin. He nodded and waved at my approach.

"This way," he said.

He stood as I approached.

"Let's go," he said.

"Where?" I asked.

He turned. "Away."

I followed him farther into the woods. Behind us I could hear voices.

"We gotta move," Clint said.

The cabin was lost from sight quickly, the woods dim and damp. We wound our way deep into a ravine then up its course. The sound of any pursuit faded as we made our way uphill.

"What are we gonna do, Clint?" I asked, coming up beside him. Ahead Latoya stood from where she'd lain in the cover of a stump.

"I wondered what happened to you," I said.

"Me and, uh, Clint came back to the cabin," she said. "Right after we got here, you showed up with the Man and we got scarce."

"Sorry to turn this into a firefight, but it looked like things weren't going your way," Clint said.

"You don't know the half of it," I said.

Off to my left suddenly came the sound of leaves and branches cracking underfoot. I turned toward it. Benny limped through the woods toward us.

"Run," I said to Latoya and Clint. "Keep going into the woods."

I turned to face Benny, who was on me in a couple of seconds. He brought a pistol to bear and stopped a few yards away.

"No further," he said, breathing hard. His skin looked gray, his eyes glassy.

"It's over," I said. "What else do you want?"

"Your asses," he said. "This bitch turned on me, this cracker asshole shot me, and you've been fucking with me for the last two days."

Clint had brought his gun around to face Benny. "Don't do it, man," Clint said.

Benny brought his pistol around and fired at Clint.

Clint dove to his right and returned fire. I closed the distance to Benny and hit him low, as he seemed to fly away from me. He went down with a cry. I was on top of him. He tried to bring the pistol toward me, his eyes wild. I grabbed his wrists and pinned his arms to the ground. After the exchange of shots the woods were suddenly deathly quiet, the only sound the grunting of our struggle.

Benny tried to kick me off. He twisted and gasped, the air steaming. Blood frothed at the edges of his mouth. I looked down and saw that he'd been shot in the chest.

"Fuck you," he said, wheezing and then coughing. His eyes grew unfocused and his struggling faded away. His breaths came unevenly then slowed. The gun fell from his grasp. The air left him in a long, rattling exhalation.

I climbed off him. Sitting beside him, I picked up the

pistol and tried to still the pounding in my chest. My stomach turned inside out and I knelt among the fallen leaves and vomited up the morning's bile and acid.

Leaves crackled again. I looked up. Clint stood over me.

He bent down and helped me to my feet. "You okay?" he asked.

"Yeah," I said. As I stood, my head swam and I teetered, grabbing on to a tree for support.

We turned to look back toward the cabin. The agents were closing through the trees, coming at us from three different points.

"We'd better go," Clint said.

I shook my head. "This is insanity," I said. "Where we gonna go to?"

Clint took a step back, then another. "I ain't going to jail," he said. "These woods go on a long way. There's lots of room to get lost."

Once again footsteps crackled through the underbrush. This time, Buendia appeared in front of us, an AR-15 on his shoulder.

"They won't be far behind us," he said. "We need to go."

"What are you doing with this guy?" I asked Clint.

"He backed me up," Clint said.

"He's a damn Cuban spy," I said. "A double agent for Castro."

Clint snorted. "Bullshit, man," he said.

"His name's not even Buendia," I said. "It's Alarcon. He's a spy. The CIA showed me his picture."

Buendia came forward. "Do not understand me too quickly," he said. "Everything I told you is true. I am going back to Havana to work for my people. Fidel is finished. Communism is finished. But the people who will be able to effect a change after the Old One is gone are not those Batista whores."

"You've been lying to us all day. Why should we believe you now?"

He drew closer, now speaking quietly. "It is all just lies. Lies within lies. The truth is never simple. Or perhaps it is too simple. The lie is always easier to deal with. I left Cuba after the revolution to avoid arrest. I kept ties to some of my officers in the army. On occasion I gave them information through third parties that would serve them and help them advance. On occasion they gave such information to me. I served the refugee community when I agreed with their ends. I waited and watched. When I heard of the collapse of the money-laundering schemes here and the rumor of the missing money, I came here quietly to see what I could learn."

"You admit you've been spying on Hartley and me for months and you want me to be happy with that?"

"Do you know why everyone wants those files? Do you know why the FBI and the CIA and the mob and the Cubans are all here? It isn't just the money. It's what's in those files. When Castro came to Havana, all the mobsters fled. But one stayed behind and was arrested—Santos Trafficante. Do you know who came to visit him while he was in jail there? Jack Ruby. Castro set Trafficante free soon afterward. He returned to Tampa, but the ties with Cuba remained. The files you have are those of his right-hand man over all those years—he saw it all, then was stupid enough to write it down after he was farmed out to the provinces to be kept quiet. You had the bad luck to stumble across this."

"What?" I asked.

"It's all in there. Thirty years of payback. Retribution against the Kennedys. Retribution from Castro for the Missile Crisis and the assassination attempts and the embargo.

Retribution from the mob for Kennedy's betrayals — they delivered West Virginia and Illinois for him, then Bobby went after them as Attorney General. They settled the score in Dallas. Oswald was their patsy. Ruby was theirs. The second gunman was theirs.

"And there's more," he went on. "In 1968. Los Angeles. They settled with Bobby. Later there were hits against Sam Giancana and others. The CIA and FBI knew more than they wanted to both before and after. Hoover knew. Johnson knew. Nixon knew. They all turned a blind eye because they were afraid Kennedy was going soft on the Russians and Vietnam, or that he was spilling secrets to his mistress who was in the pocket of the mob, or they were afraid of being caught after the fact, or they were just afraid.

"And there is still more. Now, there is a trail of money from Colombian cocaine traffickers to banks in Central America and from there to buy arms for the Contras in Nicaragua. Payments from the Medillin cartel in exchange for your government turning a blind eye to certain of their dealings — all approved at the highest levels. The Cubans, the mob, the intelligence agencies, the presidency are all involved here. Everyone wants to keep those files from seeing the light of day."

"So give them back to me and I'll make them public," I said.

He stared at me for a moment. "You think they would let you? And even if they were made public, nothing would change. There will be a few days of talking heads on the news and a few Senate hearings, and nothing will change. If you give them to the government, they will bury them. Let me keep them. With them I can be of use to my home-land."

"If it'd blow over like that, why are they afraid of it?"

"Because they are afraid of the truth and afraid that they will be the ones left twisting in the wind when the truth is revealed. They live their lives in the dark and in fear of the light. The threat of the truth being made public is far more powerful than anything that would really happen if it were."

"Won't you be arrested if you go back?"

"I have served my country after a fashion here. Castro is aware. And once I have returned, the files will give me leverage." He grabbed my arm. "You must believe this. My whole life I have moved through this swamp of lies and shit, but what I say now is the truth. I feel that only now has fate put into my hands the means to achieve some change in my country. Forces are moving. Communism's day has ended. All I ask is that you do not give me up. That is all."

I stood there with him in the woods. I looked into his eyes and away, my head spinning. Who was I to believe? What was I to do? My father had sat with me in the hotel room. Deep into a bottle, he had looked at me as I sat on the bed trying to watch television. He was trapped deep in the contradictions of his life and choices. He knew no way out and had refuge only in drink. Soon he'd be dead from his own drunken hand. I should have told him then to burn it all down and run. Get out of this miserable small-town graveyard; do anything, leave me and my mother to save your life instead of dying carelessly and randomly, as you did. Except to do that, he would have had to stop being himself, to cease being the noble man of principles that he struggled his whole life to try to be. He might have lived, but a part of him would have died. And would that have been any better?

"Go," I said to him. "Quickly. I'll stay here and slow down the Feds."

"They're going to arrest you, man," Clint said.

"Maybe, but they want to know what I know and I still

haven't given them the account numbers or the encryption key. I've got some leverage, too."

Buendia looked at me, then nodded and squeezed my arm.

I didn't know if it was the right thing to do. I didn't know what was right anymore. I was dirty and dog-tired and pulled in six different ways, but this man standing here with me seemed authentic. It was all I had to go by—a feeling in my gut.

Clint looked at Buendia as he turned to leave. "I ain't gonna be arrested," he said.

"Come with me," Buendia said. "There is work to do."

Clint bit his lip. Down the slope came the sound of people crashing through the brush. He shouldered his rifle.

"Fuck it," he said. "I'm in. I'm not even sure what for, but I'm in."

Latoya looked at them. "I ain't running into the woods with them. I take my chances with Nelson."

"Look after my place, if you can," Clint said. "I'll let you know how things go."

They turned and headed off through the woods. I looked at Latoya, who leaned wearily against a tree trunk.

"Y'all are crazy," she said. She sat down on the ground.

I sat down beside her. Benny lay sprawled out in front of us.

"How you going to explain that?" she asked.

"I have a feeling no one's going to be digging too deep into what Benny was doing here."

The agents had closed on us. Twenty yards away, they took up cover behind trees, pistols trained on us.

"Freeze!" the junior G-man said.

We looked at him incredulously. Latoya and I held up our hands limply.

Edmonds and the spook held their positions while Junior advanced on us.

"Everyone, facedown!" Junior shouted. "Spread 'em!"

"Facedown yourself," I said.

"Don't do it, Nelson!" Jack shouted.

"Go ahead, Jack, shoot me! But I ain't eating dirt for you." I held out my hands. "I'm not armed. The girl's harmless. Benny's dead."

Junior grabbed one of my hands and started to cuff me. Jack surveyed the scene. The spook walked up slowly, still holding his gun.

"Was this *necessary*, Jack?" I asked. "You gonna throw Latoya and me in jail to cover your asses until you can think of a way to shut us up? Or are you going to just see that we disappear?"

Jack glowered and kicked at the dirt. He took in the scene again, then sighed. "Let 'em go," he said to the junior G-man.

Junior looked at him.

"Let them go," he repeated.

"We can't just let these two loose," the spook said.

"They're material witnesses," Jack said, "but they're not suspects. They've cooperated with us. I see no reason to hold them."

The spook came up close to Jack and murmured something.

"Just get the fuck out of my jurisdiction," Jack said to him aloud. "I don't give a goddamn about your bullshit. As far as I can tell, this dead bastard who worked for you committed a half-dozen felonies, and you violated the Agency's charter in dealing with him. You want me to make it a federal investigation, just keep on riding me."

Junior unlocked my handcuffs and pushed me away. I helped Latoya to her feet again. The spook stood there, sizing up the situation. Finally he holstered his pistol.

"I'll be in the car," he said and headed back toward the clearing.

Jack and the junior G-man went off to make calls on their car radio. Latoya came over and sat beside me. It was cold in the early morning and she leaned into me for warmth. The sun was in the tops of the trees and the autumn leaves glowed and fluttered in a golden light.

"Sorry," she said after many minutes of sitting in silence.

"Hey, you were just another innocent victim, I guess," I said.

"We're all just victims of being born," she said.

The sun finally cleared the high hills to the east and filled the yard and the woods with light. I turned to face the sun, its warmth welcome. I stood up. I felt stiff and sore and tired and empty.

Latoya reached out a hand and I pulled her back to her feet.

EPILOGUE

I have discovered that all human evil comes from this, man's being unable to sit still in a room.

—Blaise Pascal

37

Hartley

A LIGHT filled the room and the buzzing of a valence about to go. There was the smell of antiseptics and room deodorizer covering up an under-odor of urine. I opened by eyes and a hospital room swam into focus.

Goddamnit, I was still alive.

Things sifted in and out of focus. Hard-washed cotton sheets were tucked over me and I could see my feet and could feel them too, although the main thing I felt was pain.

Lacy sat beside the hospital bed. She looked marvelous, like she did when she was thirty-five, trim and glowing, her eyes bright.

"What a goddamn mess you've made," she said, laughing at me.

"I'm always a mess without you," I said.

"You never needed me when I was alive," she said.

"You worked all day and drank all night." She laughed again.

She was right. I'd taken our time together for granted and squandered it away.

"I'm sorry. Something always seemed to get in the way."

"Don't waste your time," she said. "You spend all your time looking back. There's not much time left ahead of you. Don't spend it being a sour old fart. Don't worry about me. Look at me! I'm thirty-five."

"Isn't it nice to think so."

She just started laughing at me. It broke my heart to see her looking so marvelous. I wanted to touch her. A moment later a doctor came into the room and stood between us. I craned my neck to see around him.

"Don't go," I said. "He'll be gone in a minute."

"He's hallucinating again," he said, calling over his shoulder. "Give him five milligrams of Haldol."

"No," I said, struggling, finding my arms restrained with cloth ties.

The nurse sank the needle into my deltoid and pushed the Haldol. Lacy had left. My heart split in two.

38

Ingram

W E walked back to Clint's cabin. While the agents were on the radio trying to get the local authorities out here, I went into the cabin and took the whiskey from his kitchen. Latoya lay down on Clint's bed while I poured myself a drink.

"That your answer to everything?" she asked, watching me from the bed. "To get drunk?"

I poured three fingers' worth and shotgunned it down. "You got a better plan?"

I tossed down another two fingers of whiskey, then two more. After about twenty minutes, the first cars began to climb up the switchback road toward the cabin. From the yard the noise grew—the drone of engines, the murmur of voices, the crack and rustle of footfalls across the ground.

I took the bottle out onto the porch. Edmonds stood beside his car, trying not to listen to the spook who stood at his shoulder. He looked over and saw me standing on the porch. He nodded curtly at the spook, then headed over toward the cabin. I walked to the front steps to meet him. The whiskey must have hit me hard. I stumbled down the steps and fell to the ground as he walked up.

He knelt on one knee beside me. I looked up into his face.

"Goddamnit, Ingram," he said softly, "What the hell's up with you?"

I pushed myself up and sat in the dirt. My chest heaved and I fought back tears.

"I don't know," I said.

Jack took me by the hand and pulled me to my feet. "Christ, man," he said, "you took on the mob, the CIA, Cuban vigilantes, and Castro and lived to talk about it." He drew me close. "And you *will* talk about it."

I took a deep breath. "It's all fucked up," I said. "Everything I touch turns to shit."

"It was shit before you touched it," he said. "Who do you think you are—King Midas?"

"Thanks," I said.

He grabbed me again. "One more thing," he said. "Where's the damn notebook?"

"Oh," I said. "Slipped my mind."

"I'm sure."

"It's in the chicken coop," I said, nodding toward the chicken wire shed that housed Clint's poultry. "There's about nine inches of chicken shit on the floor there. It's underneath it in the far right corner."

Jack sighed. "Story of my fucking life," he said.

"You'll need this, too," I said, pulling the photocopy from my pocket. I handed it to him. "The account numbers in the notebook are encrypted. This is the encryption key. It might be of some use if the CIA tries to mess with you."

He unfolded the paper and looked at it. "When were you planning to tell me about this?"

"Just now."

*   *   *

WE rolled down the switchback to the highway, in the back of a sheriff's car. Latoya sat beside me and stared at me.

"I'm sorry," I said to her. "Everything's ended so badly."

She looked at me a moment longer then snorted. "Shit," she said, "I'd be dead if it weren't for you. You don't think I know that? You didn't put all that coke up my nose. You didn't send Benny to fuck me up. You did the best you could with what you had. That's better than I can say."

It was cold comfort. I sat with her as we made our way into town. She took me by the hand.

"For a white boy, you're okay," she said.

39

Hartley

THE next day the sun rose again, once again confirming nature's indifference to the pocket dramas of man. Had she any appreciation for the tragic, Mother Nature would have canceled sunshine for at least a week. What I wouldn't have given for the blissful, blind acceptance of a hound dog or a housecat or a toad. Nature was no mystery to them—they were always completely and placidly in consonance with it. What a fucking curse consciousness was—it made you just smart enough to be unhappy with what you had without quite knowing what you wanted, to ask questions you had no hope of ever answering.

So, I lay in bed, calling for morphine and Xanax and Phenergan—anything that would numb me up good. I felt desolate and sick and disgusted and sorry for myself. Everyone I'd ever loved was dead and I'd failed at revenge and then couldn't even manage to kill myself.

Some physical therapist born during the Nixon Administration came in that afternoon, put a back brace on me, and hauled me out of bed. At first I played the Grandpa with Old Timer's and pretended not to understand a word she said, but she plowed right through my stupid indifference and sat me up and slapped the brace on me. I moved on to cursing and telling her to go away, but she just smiled sweetly and chided me for saying such things in front of a young lady.

Before I knew it, she had me standing up and leaning into a walker. My legs wobbled but held. The pain in my back boiled up but didn't boil over. I took a step and then another.

We walked to the door and back, the little physical therapist cooing and gushing encouragement.

"Oooh, Dr. Hartley, you're doing great for your first time out of bed."

"Save it, honey," I said, steering for the recliner beside the bed. I settled into the chair. "My back is killing me. Tell the nurse it's time for my morphine."

She folded up the walker and smiled sweetly. "Aren't we the old grump today?" she said, then pertly left the room.

Christ. I sat back and waited for my shot. What the hell was I going to do with myself? I'd spent my whole life studying the means and manner of death, yet couldn't seem to find it for myself when it was all that I longed for. It would be a while until I could get home and lay my hands on one of my guns. I could do it like Hemingway, sitting in the front hall with two barrels in my mouth, tripping the triggers with my toes. Except that would make a horrible mess for William to clean up. But then, William was gone. Christ.

After a while, the nurse showed up with the morphine and a few minutes later more than one kind of pain started to seem academic again. I sat back and gave myself over to the grips of morphia. Jesus, it was a wonder the world wasn't knee deep in junkies. It seemed the cure for the curse of being alive.

I must have slept in the recliner, because the next thing I knew, Ingram was sitting beside me. I blinked and straightened myself.

"Hey," Nelson said, "How're you feeling?"

"Like shit, sonny," I said.

"The doctors say the strength in your legs should improve, and that if you finish your radiation treatments, things should stabilize."

"Swell," I said. The glow of the morphine was gone and my bleak future prospects seemed all too real again.

"Listen, Seymour," he said, "there's a lot I'm to blame for, but your prostate cancer isn't one of them."

"You're damn straight there's a lot you're to blame for," I said glumly. I was pissed off at the world and he just happened to be its closest representative, so why shouldn't I take it out on him?

"What can I do to help?" he said.

"Shoot me."

"Other than that."

I turned to look out the window. The sun was setting and clouds were huddling up in the west, cast orange and red. In a tall pine tree outside my window, a big pileated woodpecker flapped into view and clung to the trunk. He goggled to and fro, poked at the tree, then seemed to look at me, with his black beaded eye. He was a lordly, indifferent son-of-a-bitch.

"Don't look at me, old man," he seemed to be saying. "I didn't put all those notions in your head."

I turned back to Nelson. He looked a mess, unkempt and unwashed and ghostly, asking what he could do to help me. We were a sorry pair, but he did owe me a few and

looked like he needed something to do. And, Lord knows,
I could use a hand.

I sighed.

"Get me out of here, son," I said.

40

THEY took us to the Litchfield P.D. and questioned us separately for hours. They'd turned Latoya loose with no strings attached—I imagined they didn't want anyone to know too much about what had gone on with Benny—but they asked me to stick around for a few days. We stood together outside the police department.

"What are you gonna do?" I asked.

She nodded her head toward the bus station that sat a few blocks down the street. "Guess I'll head back to L.A. and do what I can to get Reggie back."

"I think the FBI got the knapsack with the money in it. Otherwise I'd let you have it," I said.

She shook her head. "Had enough of that shit. Nothing good ever came from it. Blood money."

A police cruiser pulled up in front of us on the street.

"The cops are gonna give me a ride back to the motel to get my bag," she said.

"Good luck," I said.

She smiled painfully, "Yeah. Sure. Can't get much more bad luck."

The cop behind the wheel honked his horn and glowered at us through the window.

She stepped down. "Take care," she said.

I nodded. There had been nothing between us except a shared history of disaster, but even that had created a bond I didn't want to let go. She climbed into the car and in another moment she was gone.

I stood there on the curb, tired, dirty, hungry, demoralized, and still half-drunk. The day was growing old, the air cool. High up in the blue, jet contrails froze up in the stratosphere, crisscrossing the sky. The town of my father lay all around me, peaceful, unperturbed, oblivious.

Across the town square, Uncle Rayburn was sitting in his hardware store. Down the street at the newspaper, Leyland Parish was busy closing up shop after putting out the day's edition. The good citizens came and went on the sidewalks. None of them knew or even guessed what goes on in the world and they wouldn't want to hear it if I tried to tell them.

What was I to do? Another beautiful autumn day was drawing to a close. Though the hospital was a couple of miles away, I decided to walk there and see how Hartley was doing. I was finished with leaning on others.

When I got there, it was almost dusk. I made my way up the elevators and found Hartley's room. He was sitting up in a recliner. His color was better, but he looked terribly drawn and depressed.

He sniped and crabbed at me for a while. I let him go on, for it seemed to make him feel better. Finally, I asked him, "Seymour, what are you going to do? How can I be of help to you?"

He turned to look out the window. "Get me out of here," he said.

"Do you want to go home?"

He thought about it for a moment. "I don't think I want to go back there," he said at last.

"Where, then?"

The light was almost gone from the sky.

"Someplace warm," he said.

My hands were in my pockets. I felt the key Buendia had given me to the safe house in the Gulf.

I nodded. "Okay," I said, "I'll take care of things. Everything will be all right."

He seemed to relax back into his chair when he heard this. The furrows on his brow flattened out and he exhaled deeply.

"Sometimes it's nice to believe that," he said.

About the Author

Stephen J. Clark is an M.D. who has lived in California, Oregon, Massachusetts, Florida, and Alabama. He now lives in North Carolina with his wife and children. He has published short stories in several regional publications, as well as essays in medical journals. His research on infectious diseases was featured in *Time* magazine and *USA Today*.

Life may seem simple in Litchfield, Alabama,
but murder certainly isn't...

SOUTHERN
LATITUDES

by

Stephen J. Clark

0-425-18637-7

*Nelson Ingram left Alabama a young man full of
promise and ambition. Now a burnt-out
disillusioned reporter, he has come back to the one
place he's avoided for most of his adult life—his
home town of Litchfield. Unfortunately, it's exactly
how he left it...*

Available wherever books are sold or
to order call 1-800-788-6262